WORLD
UPSIDE DOWN

WORLD UPSIDE DOWN

The Life of Paul, God's Chosen Messenger

Louis McCall

Library of Congress Control Number: 2024903999

ISBN: 979-8-89228-092-1   (Paperback)
ISBN: 979-8-89228-100-3   (eBook)

Printed in the United States of America

The cover picture is of a section of the wall of old Damascus, Syria that has been preserved. The partially bricked over window is the place where Paul is believed to have been let down in a large basket to escape those seeking to take his life. The cast metal statue nearby represents Paul falling from his horse on the road to Damascus in his encounter with the resurrected Lord Jesus Christ.

DEDICATION

This book is dedicated to God the Holy Spirit who put it in me to write this book. I didn't think I was up to the task or know whether it should be a single book or several volumes. I just began writing and relied on the Holy Spirit for guidance.

I also want to dedicate this book to the memory of the apostle Paul of Tarsus. I gained a new understanding of Paul, the challenges, and obstacles that he faced, and his dogged determination to fulfill the assignment he received directly from the Lord Jesus Christ.

Paul had no detailed blueprint. The scriptures, the words of Jesus during his earthly ministry, and Paul's encounters with the resurrected Christ in visions, along with the guidance and one on one teaching of the Holy Spirit, and angelic messengers, were his marching orders, signs, and confirmations. The rest was a walk of faith. His itinerary was determined by the leading of the Holy Spirit. He organized the network of churches that he set up, revisited them like a circuit rider, assembled a multinational evangelistic team of men and women, Hebrews and former pagans, appointed leaders, and gave detailed instructions through his letters on how to worship God, preserve apostolic teaching, maintain discipline, and be ready to suffer for the gospel.

Paul was tough as nails. He endured multiple beatings, a stoning, evaded conspiracies to kill him, survived satanic schemes to take his life, and, in the end, boldly faced martyrdom. By his perseverance, witness, and demonstration of the power of God, he, along with others, turned the world upside down.

ACKNOWLEDGMENTS

The King James Version of the Holy Bible served as the source book for this fictional account. Although fictional, this book is based on what is recorded in the Bible. Where dialogue is taken from the Bible, it was paraphrased by the author into modern colloquial English. Other dialogue comes from the artistic license of the author and is fictional.

Scripture quotations are from The Authorized (King James) Version. Rights in the Authorized Version in the United Kingdom are vested in the Crown and are reproduced by permission of the Crown's patentee, Cambridge University Press.

I also want to acknowledge the helpful assistance of Barbara Hollace, Cassandra Johnson, and Tarinna Olley. Their sage advice and sharp eyes contributed greatly to improving this book.

ENDORSEMENTS

One of the most important questions in life is to ask: Who should be my teachers? Louis McCall is not just an author who has an interest in the Scriptures. Louis is a man of prayer and God's Word who passionately lives out and applies the Scripture in His daily life. He is a man of integrity and wisdom. He is a needed voice, and I would submit, he is a worthy teacher.

I hope you will receive the teaching in *World Upside Down* as he walks us through the life of one of the most influential disciples of Christ in world history. Partake of his creative imagination in retelling the story. He doesn't just share a narrative; he draws out the miraculous transformation that inspires the human soul. You will continually be confronted with a man who was redeemed and became an activator of faith to so many around him. So much so, his identity was literally changed (from Saul to Paul).

Louis doesn't just tell a story from books; he walks us through the literal historical sites of many of the settings of this bold and powerful storyline. As you read, as you receive, I pray you too would consider all that God can do in and through you, with a trust and active faith in Christ.

Joel Schmidgall
Executive Pastor, National Community Church
Washington, D.C.

✦ ✦ ✦

Louis McCall successfully takes on the challenge of telling the Apostle Paul's 'upside down' story, a story that made no sense to the people of his day. The author attempts to help the reader make sense of Paul, his life, his choices, and experiences with a unique literary license that remains true to the holy scriptures yet provides insight into what the Apostle was thinking and experiencing. With strategically placed photographs and masterful biblical literacy, Louis demonstrates a well-seasoned life of professorship and a long and full political career. Experience Paul through a seasoned lens that helps us to understand God's plan of love, grace, and mercy to a broken, needy, and desperate world.

Bob McGurty, PhD
President and Chairman, Calcutta Mercy
Kolkata, West Bengal, India

✦ ✦ ✦

I loved reading *World Upside Down*. In this day and age, one needs sound biblical teaching and the right books that can point us to the Lord Jesus Christ and the message of salvation. When the disciples asked Jesus in Matthew chapter 24 about the end of the age, He told them in verse 4 to be careful that no man deceive them. Deception and ignorance of Biblical truth is one of the signs of the times.

What I appreciated most about *World Upside Down* is that Louis McCall has taken the history, story, and theology of the Apostle Paul and the early church and presented it to readers in an authentic, interesting, and creative way to a public that is fast losing the knowledge of the Word of God. I particularly enjoyed learning about the history of Middle Eastern countries that Paul visited and was fascinated by the current pictures of such places which have been included in the narrative. This made the book come alive for me, a modern reader. Refreshingly, *World Upside Down* is true to the Word of God but also contains literary creativity that gives readers context and understanding of the life and ministry of Paul during the times of the early church.

I highly endorse this book and the creative, but true to the Word, artistry of Louis McCall.

Tina Mdobilu
Co-Pastor, Tanzania Assemblies of God,
Manzese "B" Church, Dar es Salaam, Tanzania
Co-Founder, Prayer Mountain Ministries, Houston, Texas

✦ ✦ ✦

This book on the life of Paul, *World Upside Down*, is really a great effort. The story it tells is of the transformation from Saul to Paul beginning with his encounter with God. This encounter made the difference in his life. Saul was a person who scattered and slaughtered the church. But Paul was a missionary, a man who carried the Gospel with obedience and commitment. Paul's life is a model role for the servant of God, and this book illustrates that perfectly. When we encounter God, He changes our direction and legacy, and we become a resilient disciple and missionary before our Lord. We don't seek our own desires but follow God's plan for us. As the book brings out, Paul was a witness in all circumstances. His testimony impacted on Mark's and many others' lives. Even while he was imprisoned, he never stopped being on mission. I appreciate Louis for sharing the wonderful writings of this book, *World Upside Down*. May it touch many hearts and change their lives. God bless you!

Bishop Qamar Aziz
Independent Evangelistic Outreach Ministries
Punjab, Pakistan

✦ ✦ ✦

Masterful storytelling… for such an intricate character. The author brings Paul's magnanimous life to a level that we all can understand and relate to. The creative dialogues will keep you engaged and transport you to the very beginnings of the "followers of The Way."

Themes of grace, righteousness, community, and perseverance are brilliantly captured throughout the narratives. If you want a fresh understanding of Paul, you will appreciate this concise book.

Kelvin Mulembe
Pastor, Arlington Temple United Methodist Church
Arlington, Virginia

✦ ✦ ✦

It has been such a pleasure to literally absorb this book and to be compelled to keep inculcating the pure Word of God written with such verve and abandonment to the truth. The characters shine through with immense design, and it has been a huge honor to not just read with understanding but also insight and to pick up all the minuscule detail provided. This book forms clarification needed in these very high-stress times we are enduring.

Philip P. DeVries
Chairman, Life Enterprises
George, Western Cape, Republic of South Africa

✦ ✦ ✦

Dr. Louis McCall, the profound Professor, dynamic Diplomat, and awesome Ambassador for our Savior, Lord, and Liberator Jesus Christ, took the pen of his creativity, dipped it into the inkwell of his anointed imagination and brilliantly penned this fictional\semi-biographic work covering the life, the call, and the legacy of the Apostle Paul.

Embedded in this wonderful work one will witness great biblical truths and see the awesome hand of GOD as HE transforms "a Pharisee among Pharisees," Saul of Tarsus, into the articulate Apostle Paul. You will experience his conversion as well as his overcoming the forces and counterforces that sought to prevent the completion of Paul's mission and mandate from GOD.

xiv

World Upside Down takes the reader along the life path of the Apostle as he builds churches, preaches and teaches, endures storms and shipwrecks, and suffers a potentially deadly snakebite all while writing nearly two thirds of the New Testament, the foundation upon which the modern church is built.

Upon reading this well written work and labor of love, one can take comfort in knowing that if you know GOD for yourself through Jesus Christ, just as with Saul, GOD will meet you right where you are, no matter what your condition and despite all opposition, He will place you in position to carry out HIS divine mission.

This is an excellent read and it is a high honor and precious privilege to endorse this book. I pray that you enjoy it as much as I did.

Robert A. Woods, Pastor
The Historic Berean Baptist Church
Washington, D.C.

CONTENTS

CHAPTER 1

The Second Roman Imprisonment

As was his daily discipline, Paul the Apostle, woke early, prayed, and got into the presence of God. After he performed his morning ablutions,he set about singing hymns of praise to God and offering up additional prayers for the churches he had planted and for those faithful men and women he put in place to oversee those churches. As the morning light entered his private dwelling, a residence made possible by the gifts of the saints, he also read from scrolls of the Tanakh. He had memorized much of the Tanakh from his early days as a Pharisee and student of the Holy Scriptures.

Paul preferred to be going about his travels revisiting the churches he and his team had planted and setting up new churches that would come into being from his preaching. He preached the message of salvation through repentance of sin and faith in the person and work of Jesus Christ, the very Son of God who was one with Father God and God the Holy Spirit.

Unfortunately, after being acquitted and released from Roman imprisonment under the young Emperor Caesar Nero a few years earlier, Paul was eventually placed in custody again and brought back to Rome in chains. Nevertheless, he was allowed to arrange for his own lodging with his freedom constrained by Roman soldiers who chained themselves to Paul's manacles. The irony of the situation was that Paul, by this arrangement, had a personal protective detail against those Jews that rejected Jesus as the Christ and sought to kill him in order to permanently silence him. The guards were changed or relieved periodically. This provided Paul with a new captive audience with each change.

Another Soldier Open to the Gospel Message

On this day the new guard presented himself. "Hello, my name is Marcus," said the guard. The outgoing guard confirmed that he was now giving Marcus charge of the prisoner Paul. Once they were alone, Marcus removed his helmet, set his shield aside, and informed Paul, "Sir, I have made arrangements to be the sole guard with you for as long as I desire and have relieved others of this charge until such time as I ask to be relieved."

"Why," Paul asked, "do you want to experience the life of a prisoner of Rome?"

Marcus replied, "I have heard from other recent guards having this duty, as well as from others who spent time with you during your previous confinement in Rome, of the things you shared with them and I have seen how it has changed their lives. Many, including some in the elite Imperial Pretorian Guard, have become followers of The Way that you teach. Even when you were imprisoned in Philippi, a city of Macedonia where many Roman military veterans retire with special privileges, the Imperial Guard, also called the Pretorian Guard, heard of you and your radical message. So, if you will, please tell me the whole of your story from the beginning."

Welcome Visitors

"Why of course, Marcus," said Paul. Just then a group of some of Paul's regular visitors, including Luke, a physician and a steadfast co-laborer in Paul's journeys, together with Eubulus, Pudens, Linus, and Claudia came in bearing food and drink. They halted upon seeing Marcus. "These are friends of mine, Marcus," said Paul. "Be at ease." Addressing the visitors, Paul said, "It is always a blessing to see all of you."

Luke responded, "We have brought you fresh water, wine, bread, cheeses, grapes, dates, and some dried fish."

"Please," said Paul, "let's all, including my new friend Marcus here, enjoy this meal together."

"If you wish," said Claudia, "but only a little. It is a small offering for you." Paul took the still warm bread in one hand and the wineskin in the other. Lifting them up to heaven Paul prayed, "Most gracious Lord Jesus, we first of all take this bread and wine in remembrance of Your suffering for our redemption with Your blood and body as the Lamb of God, the acceptable sacrifice to God our Father that takes away our sin."

After Paul and his visitors shared that solemn moment, sharing the wine and bread, they then took part in the gifts of food. Turning to Marcus, Paul said, "You are welcome to partake of the regular food, but the portion of the wine and bread we just shared is part of a holy remembrance that is only for believers in Jesus Christ."

After sharing in the meal and bringing Paul up to date on the status of the believers in Rome, Luke and the others departed. But before departing, Luke said, "Paul, your second letter to Timothy, that you wrote from this place, has been received by Timothy. I found a trusted believer who was about to sail for Ephesus and gave it to him charging him to deliver it to Timothy at the church in Ephesus. He did so and returned recently. I believe Timothy and Mark will come soon, arriving before winter, with your heavy cloak, books, and parchments you requested."

Paul was encouraged by the good news and blessed his visitors as they took their leave. "Now, Marcus, regarding your request, allow me to begin at my beginning," said Paul.

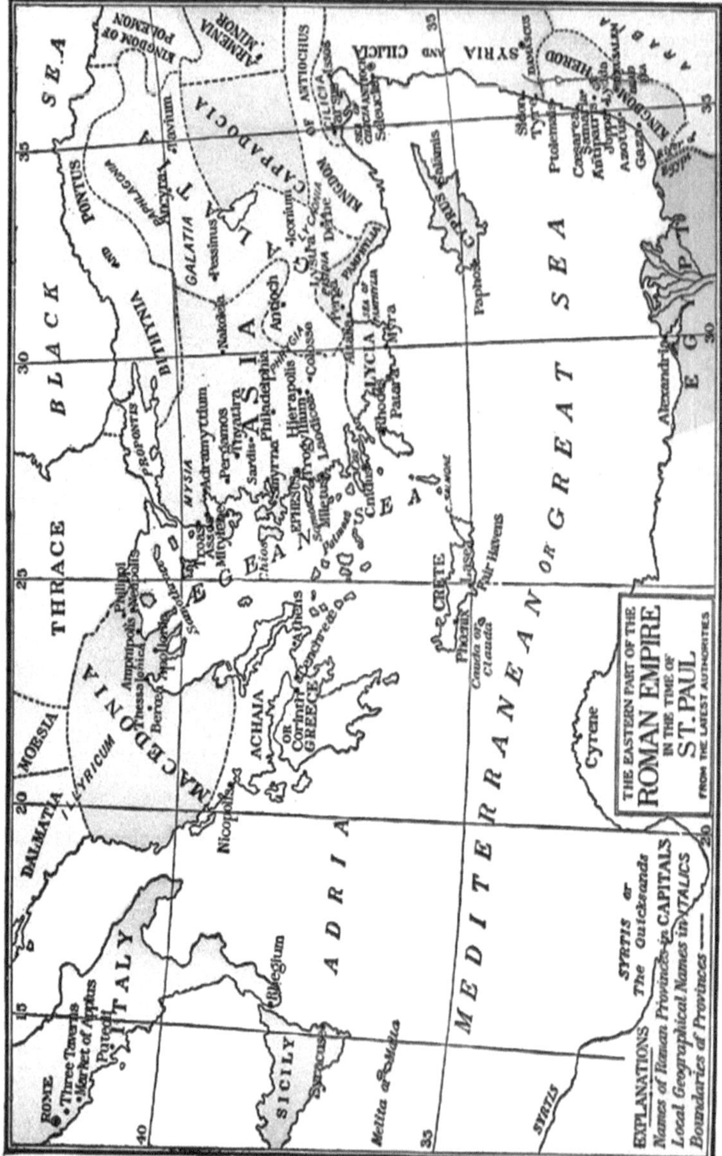

Eastern Part of the Roman Empire in the Time of Saint Paul
Map used courtesy of the Florida Center for Instructional Technology, College of Education, University of South Florida. From the private collection of Roy Winkelman. https://etc.usf.edu/maps

CHAPTER 2

From Legalism and the Law to Faith, Grace, and the Blood of Jesus

Origins of Saul

Paul began to reveal to Marcus the story of his own life. "Marcus," Paul said, "I was born a Roman citizen in Tarsus of the Province of Cilicia in the final years of the reign of Caesar Augustus. I am also a Jew. I traced my lineage to the tribe of Benjamin, and my Jewish name was Saul, in honor of the first king of Israel, who, like me, was a Benjaminite. I was raised according to the strictest sect of the Jews. I prided myself in being a Pharisee among Pharisees. I wore the outward signs of being an observant Pharisee with my leather phylacteries binding foundational portions of scripture to my left arm and the same in a leather box strapped to my forehead. Likewise, the fringed borders of my garments, along with my prayer shawl, signified my Jewish identity as a Pharisee. At the time, I was prideful in that."

Marcus interrupted, "But why don't you wear those now? Are you no longer a Jew?"

Paul explained, "I am most certainly a Jew, and I don't deny my heritage in that regard. However, my true identity is with the Lord Jesus Christ whose Spirit lives in me. I have also determined to be all things to all people that I might save some who would thereby give heed to my testimony.

"My Jewish father saw that I was raised in our traditions. I memorized much of our scriptures, beginning with the Torah. I was also trained in the trade of my father. Because Tarsus is a notable city in the empire and a seaport, I learned Greek and some Latin because

Tarsus was a cosmopolitan crossroads. Knowledge of Greek and Latin was necessary to do business in that city and with the masters of the ships that brought their cargoes to Tarsus and then loaded up with our goods.

"When Tiberius ruled as Caesar, my father sent me to Jerusalem, in the Roman Province of Judea, to study with respected rabbis. I studied under Rabbi Gamaliel, who was the grandson of Rabbi Hillel. As I studied at the feet of Rabbi Gamaliel, I became expert in the uncompromising law of the Jews. I was so zealous in the belief that I was living according to the law of God and the traditions of our elders that I despised the people that followed John the Baptist and Rabbi Jesus. I considered them to be heretics. Rabbi Gamaliel's school was the most sought-after school of up-and-coming Pharisees.

"Although I was not a member of the Sanhedrin, a body of elders presided over by the high priest and first established by Moses in centuries past, my association with Rabbi Gamaliel opened the door for me to sit on the margins of meetings of the Sanhedrin. I was considered to be in training as a possible member of the successor generation of members of the Sanhedrin."

The Beginnings of Persecution

"After the Sanhedrin tried Jesus the Nazarene and prevailed upon Pontius Pilate, the Roman Procurator who governed Judea under Tiberius Caesar, to have Jesus crucified, I sought to increase my favor with the Sanhedrin by persecuting the followers of Rabbi Jesus. At the time, I did not realize that Jesus was the Messiah, the Christ of God, and was Himself God. I did think it strange that the Sanhedrin could not produce the body of Jesus to prove that He did not rise from the dead as He said He would. Twice the Sanhedrin ordered the arrest of Peter and John, two who had been in the inner circle of the followers of Jesus. The Sanhedrin firmly commanded Peter and John not to preach that Jesus was the risen Son of God. Upon their second arrest, the temple guards under the high priest were careful not to rough up Peter and John publicly for fear they would be stoned to death by the people.

"The high priest himself questioned Peter and John. Peter and John spoke so eloquently and fearlessly of their understanding that Jesus, whom the Jews had killed, was indeed the Christ and that only He could forgive sins. At first, I was amazed. I had studied for years under my Rabbi Gamaliel, and yet these mere fishermen from the unlearned countryside of Galilee, spoke words that pricked our hearts. It was clear that the effect of being with Jesus made them powerful voices in witness to their claims. I was so angry that I and the members of the Sanhedrin wanted to kill them on the spot without a trial.

"My Rabbi Gamaliel, who was a member of the Sanhedrin and well respected, stood up and took charge of the situation. Gamaliel was a commanding figure with his long white beard and the dress of a Pharisee. He ordered Peter and John to be taken aside so that the Sanhedrin could confer among themselves. Rabbi Gamaliel counseled to let Peter and John alone on the basis that if their doctrine was of man it would fail as history had shown with others who led uprisings. But, if the doctrine of Peter and John was of God, the Sanhedrin would fail and might be found to be fighting against God.

"The Sanhedrin took Rabbi Gamaliel's advice, but flogged Peter and John before releasing them, and sternly forbid that they should speak as representatives of Jesus or to speak about Jesus. I was confused. My Rabbi Gamaliel was saying that maybe Jesus of Nazareth was indeed the Christ. I was troubled by the words of Peter and John, but I was determined to challenge their teaching. Our whole system of worship was based on the Law of Moses and the daily sacrifices made at our beautiful Temple in Jerusalem. Yet Peter and John were not hindered by the flogging they endured or the directive of the high priest. Instead, they would come to the Temple daily to teach and proclaim Jesus as the Christ and alive from the dead.

"They taught that the blood of Jesus atoned for sin, not the burnt sacrifices offered up by the priests at the temple. They called on the people to repent of their sins and their part in the crucifixion of Jesus, believe in Jesus and by the grace of Jesus they would be found acceptable to God. This ran totally opposite of all that I had ever studied and believed. Yet, the numbers of those following this doctrine they called The Way grew day by day. It was a challenge to the system that came down from Moses. It ran contrary to the teaching of the scribes and priests. It also overturned the economy of the Temple sacrifices from which the high priests profited.

"I noticed that the number of sacrifices began to tail off as this new doctrine spread. There were even a large number of Levite priests that attached themselves to The Way. Thus, when Stephen, one of seven men appointed by Peter, John and the other principal followers of Jesus, to meet the administrative needs of their growing following, began to do miraculous things, like as was said of Jesus, a conspiracy of lies was hatched against him by those who rejected the notion that Jesus was the Messiah. These rejectionists held to the traditional way of our faith. They had Stephen arrested and brought before the Sanhedrin. The liars in this conspiracy accused Stephen of all manner of things and alleged Stephen spoke against the Temple and against the Law of Moses.

"Oddly, as the fake charges were brought against Stephen, his countenance was angelic in its serenity. When the high priest asked Stephen whether the charges made against him were true, Stephen responded, using the scriptures and beginning with our ancestor Abraham.

"The chamber was silent as Stephen spoke at length until he put us in the same camp as those who killed the prophets and now had murdered Jesus. Stephen mocked our reverence for the Law of Moses rightly saying we did not obey that law. We were so convicted and infuriated that the accusers rushed on Stephen and would have torn him apart.

"When Stephen looked up into heaven he proclaimed, 'Look! I see heaven opened and the Son of Man standing at the right hand of God!' With that they dragged Stephen out of the city to stone him. All the while the mob yelled as loud as possible to drown out Stephen's words and they put their hands over theirs ears so they would not hear anything else Stephen would say. I stood by approving as they left their clothes at my feet as they turned to stone Stephen. "As they stoned Stephen, he commended his spirit to Jesus. Then, falling to his knees under the onslaught of stones, Stephen cried out in a loud voice. He appeared to be looking straight at me while I stood on a nearby knoll, 'Lord, don't charge them for this sin! Don't lay this sin on them!' he said, and then he died.

"Although I did not stone Stephen, I was consenting in his death. It troubled me for a while, especially how Stephen prayed for those who stoned him to death. But I dealt with it by deciding to persecute and bring to the Sanhedrin all who, like Stephen, believed in this doctrine of The Way."

CHAPTER 3

From Spiritually Blind and Deaf
to Hearing the Voice of God and Seeing Visions

Believers in Jesus Scatter

B"So, initially you did not follow Jesus or believe that Jesus was from God?" asked Marcus.

"That is correct," said Paul. "That is only one of the reasons why I am the least of the apostles. The truth is I was aware of the message of Jesus and of his followers, but I dared not be seen at their gatherings, to investigate, for fear people would say that I too was a follower. I also was so set on what I had learned as a Pharisee that I could not receive the truth, due to my hardened heart. It could not take root in me. Like those who stopped their ears at the stoning of Stephen, I had willingly made myself spiritually deaf to the truth of God. Even after the crucifixion of Jesus, when Peter and John would daily come boldly to the temple to teach and preach the good news that God had sent his only son, in the person of Jesus, to be the savior of the world, I would stand out of sight, but listen to find something I might charge them with before the Sanhedrin. But their words and testimony did not get past my defenses to enter my heart and take root.

"With the permission and encouragement of the Sanhedrin, after the stoning of Stephen, I went from house to house in Jerusalem and nearby towns dragging forth men and women who were followers of The Way. They were consigned to prison to be judged by the Sanhedrin. Because this was a matter of our religion, the Roman governor stayed out of this situation, and we had a free hand. Others that were likewise zealous for the Law of Moses and Temple sacrifices assayed to do likewise. The result was that followers of The Way fled. In so doing they taught their messages in the cities and towns where they had fled or passed through in their flight."

"That is grim, but at the same time amusing," said Marcus. "You were furiously trying to stamp out The Way, but your very actions were causing it to spread."

"You are very perceptive," said Paul. "That is exactly what happened. Knowing that a great many of them sought refuge in Damascus, I determined to go to Syria and, using the same tactics as I used in Jerusalem, it was my intention to go house to house, if necessary, dragging out men and women followers of The Way, to take them bound back to Jerusalem to appear before the Sanhedrin. I asked for and received letters from the Sanhedrin that I could present to the synagogues in Damascus. Those letters gave me authority to put in chains, as many as I determined to be followers of The Way and of faith in Jesus and return with them bound to Jerusalem to be dealt with."

The Life-Changing Encounter with Jesus

"However, things took a dramatic turn that I did not anticipate. As I traveled toward Damascus with my companions, I was struck by a great light from heaven. It startled the horse I was riding such that I fell to the ground. I was dazed by the bright light and by the fall from my horse. Then I heard a voice call my name. The voice said, 'Saul, Saul, why are you persecuting me?' 'Who are you, Sir?' I asked. The voice responded, 'I am Jesus, the one you are persecuting.' Then Jesus said, 'Isn't it painfully hard for you to kick against the pricks to your conscience?'

"I was astounded and undone. Just as my Rabbi Gamaliel had cautioned, I was found fighting against God Himself. I was trembling and convicted of my errors. Realizing I had sinned against God, I said, 'Lord, what do You want me to do?'

"The Lord Jesus said, 'Get up. Go into the city, and you will be told what you have to do.'

"The men that traveled with me didn't know what to make of these happenings. They heard the voice that spoke with me but did not clearly understand the words spoken and saw no man. As I got up from the ground where I fell, I realized I could not see. The men with me took me by the hand, brushed the dust of the road off my garments, and led me on into Damascus. I remained in Damascus a blind man. For three days, I would not eat or drink. Instead, I prayed and fasted waiting for the instructions Jesus told me I would receive. Although I could not see with my natural eyes, the Lord gave me a closed eye vision of a man named Ananias coming to me and putting his hand on me that I should receive my sight again.

"As I had seen in the vision, the man Ananias came to the place I was staying in Damascus on the street called Straight, because it was just that, straight. Putting his hands on me, Ananias said, 'Brother Saul, the Lord, yes Jesus Himself, who appeared to you on the road as you were traveling to Damascus, has sent me, so that you might receive your sight again and be filled with the Holy Ghost.'

"Immediately, cloudy white discs fell from my eyes and I could see again. My heart was changed and I was filled with the Holy Spirit. It was night, but I agreed with Ananias that I should immediately go to a pool nearby to be baptized, which he did. We then returned to my lodging where I finally had something to eat and drink.

Author on Straight Street in Damascus, Syria at the Remains of a Roman Era Arch.

"I was overwhelmed by the thought that I had seen the light of the holiness of God, heard and spoken with Jesus Christ, the Son of God who took away my sins, which were many, and rose from the dead as the resurrected Lord and now abides in heaven. Moreover, the Holy Spirit now indwelt me."

CHAPTER 4

From Persecuting Followers of Jesus to Preaching the Good News of Salvation by Faith in the Person, Work, and Blood of Jesus the Christ

*T*he Persecutor becomes the Proclaimer

"So, Jesus came back from the dead and is alive in heaven?" asked Marcus. "Yes, Marcus," said Paul. "Jesus came down from heaven, was born like us, but of a virgin by the Holy Ghost as the Son of God. He lived a blameless life going about doing good. He taught the words of life. He ultimately died for the sins of the world as the only offering for sin acceptable to God and rose from the dead with the promise that He will bring all who believe in Him to life after death to be with Him in heaven eternally."

"That is a lot to digest," said Marcus.

"Indeed" said Paul, "but it is a simple message so straight forward that even a child can understand it.

"I spent a few days in the house of Ananias. Ananias introduced me to some of the disciples that dwelt in Damascus. At first, they were afraid of me because they knew I had been a persecutor of The Way and they feared I was setting a trap for them. I could see it in their faces and the whispers between them as well as their repeated glances out of the window to scan the street for unwelcome guests. But Ananias told them how God had spoken to him concerning me. After being received by my new brothers and sisters in The Way, I immediately went out about Damascus preaching in the synagogues that Jesus is the Christ and that he is the Son of God.

It was a sensation to say the least. Those that heard me in the synagogues, which included some who had recently fled Jerusalem to avoid my reign of terror, said among themselves, 'Isn't this the man that destroyed those in Jerusalem that called on the name of Jesus and has come here to track us down and take us in chains back to Jerusalem to be judged by the chief priests of the Sanhedrin?'

"It was a battle to gain their confidence. In addition, there were some rejectionist traditional Jews in Damascus that were not of The Way. These disputed with me in the synagogues, but I gave convincing proofs from the prophets and other holy scriptures in the Tanakh that this Jesus was indeed the Messiah, the very Christ of God."

The First Assassination Plot

"As the days wore on, many came to the synagogues to hear me and accepted my preaching and defense, using the scriptures, that Jesus was indeed the Christ and had risen from the dead before returning to heaven. However, those Jews that rejected Jesus Christ and held to the old way would have none of it. Although they could not successfully dispute with me in the synagogues, they conspired to kill me. They posted assassins at the city gates, both day and night, so they might kill me to silence my message and my witness. I became aware of this plot as also did the disciples in Damascus.

"The disciples let me down from the city wall of Damascus in a large basket one night and I safely made my way to the Arabian Kingdom of the Nabateans, near the Dead Sea. I bypassed Judea and I did not stop in Jerusalem, where by now I was a wanted man by the Sanhedrin. And I did not confer with the apostles in Jerusalem. Instead, I journeyed south from Damascus to Bozrah, a city built by the Nabateans. There I recalled that the prophet Isaiah, speaking of Jesus Christ to come and his blood that would be shed said, 'Who is this coming out of Edom with dyed garments from Bozrah? Who is glorious in His apparel, travelling in great strength? It is I that speak in righteousness, and I am mighty to save.' Afterwards, I continued farther south and below the Dead Sea to Petra, the capital of the

Arabian Kingdom of the Nabateans. That kingdom, unlike Judea, was independent and not part of the Roman Empire, although its ruler, King Aretas IV, had some authority in Damascus, which was part of the Roman Province of Syria-Cilicia Phoenice, but at one time was part of the expanded Arabian Kingdom of the Nabateans. Both Bozrah and Petra were built by the Nabateans who were expert in carving buildings from stone."

The Ruins of a Street in Bozrah from the Time of Paul, but Currently Located in Southern Syria and now called Basra.

The Training of an Apostle by God the Holy Spirit

"I abode in that part of Arabia for three years. I spent a lot of time alone in the desert. My companion and teacher during that time was God the Holy Spirit. There I received visions and heard the voice of God. The Spirit showed me the ministry and teaching of Jesus. I was even able to see the last Passover supper Jesus shared with his disciples the night he was betrayed, as though I were present in the room when it happened.

Although I had spent years in Tarsus and later in Jerusalem under my former Rabbi Gamaliel, what I learned from the Holy Spirit opened my eyes more clearly to Christ spoken of by the prophets. I had no need to seek out the apostles or others for understanding. God the Holy Spirit was my teacher.

"One day, while I was in prayer, I was caught up to the third heaven, that is beyond the clouds, beyond the stars, and into the third heaven where God has His throne. There I heard words that are not permitted for a flesh and blood man to utter. The Spirit also revealed to me the things I was going to suffer for the name of Jesus. I prepared myself in prayers and with fasting for the ministry I had been called to minister among the pagans beyond Judea, yet I purposed in my heart not to neglect the message of Jesus among my own Jewish brethren."

CHAPTER 5

From Myopic Jewish Nationalism to God's Vision for the World

"After three years in Arabia of the Nabateans, I returned to Damascus. There, the believers warmly received me, and I again preached in the synagogues with an even stronger message of the name of Jesus because of what I had been taught and had revealed to me by the Holy Spirit while in the Arabian Kingdom of the Nabateans. Then I returned to Jerusalem."

"I returned to Jerusalem with some trepidation. It was my first time in Jerusalem since I had left with letters from the high priests giving me authority to go to the synagogues in Damascus in Syria and bring back to Jerusalem, bound, those who had become followers of The Way. When I returned to Jerusalem, I attempted to join the disciples of that city, but they feared me, understandably, and believed I intended to entrap them under the false guise of being a disciple, so that they could be arrested and brought before the Sanhedrin. However, Barnabas brought me to the apostles and told them how I had seen the Lord on the road to Damascus, and that I had spoken to the risen Lord and went on to boldly preach the name of Jesus in Damascus."

Another Plot to Silence Paul by Assassination

"I was ultimately accepted in Jerusalem among the believers and went in and out among the disciples. While I was there, I spent fifteen days with Peter and had visits with James the brother of Jesus. In that time, I didn't see any of the other apostles. The Greek speaking Jews in Jerusalem, who like myself were raised in parts of the Roman Empire outside of Judea and in the Greek culture of language and philosophy, disputed with me as I preached in the name of Jesus. They held to the old way of being acceptable to God based on the Law of Moses, animal sacrifices for sin, and following the traditions of the elders. Jesus Himself rebuked those that, thinking themselves religious, accepted the traditions of the elders on the least of things yet did not obey the commandments of God. These people rejected the truth that I and the other apostles preached. The rejectionist traditionalists were especially stirred up against me because I had been one of them and now disputed with them. As happened in Damascus, these Jews conspired to kill me. When the disciples at Jerusalem learned of this conspiracy, they took me to Caesarea and put me on a vessel to Tarsus.

The Author and his wife Lenora at the Treasury in Petra, the Historic Capital of the Arabian Kingdom of the Nabateans, now Located in the Modern Hashemite Kingdom of Jordan.

"Tarsus was a homecoming for me, but neither I nor my message was received. I was physically attacked by leaders of the synagogues there and flogged at the direction of those leaders. It was a dry time that tested my resolve. Because the Holy Spirit had shown me the things I would suffer, I took my suffering as an honor. After all, the prophet Isaiah, speaking of the Messiah, said, 'He came to his own, but his own people would not receive him.' Knowing that Jesus is Lord, and I was his servant, I could not expect better treatment than what He received. He was unjustly flogged and crucified, after being punched and slapped by the Temple guards of the high priest as well as by the Roman soldiers. He suffered as the Just One for the unjust."

Marcus asked, "Did you ever doubt, especially since you were rejected, and your life was in danger?"

Paul answered, "It was not possible to doubt. I would repeatedly return to my encounter with the Lord Jesus Christ on the Road to Damascus and the revelations I received after that.

"Since the time of Augustus Caesar, the area of Cilicia and Syria was renamed Syria-Cilicia Phoenice, by his decree. After my return to Tarsus, I went about the regions of Cilicia and Syria. There the churches of Jewish believers in Christ did not know me by my face. They had only heard that the one who, in the past, had persecuted those in The Way now preached the faith that he had tried to destroy. Thus, they glorified God for what He had done in me."

The Controversy of Salvation Coming to Pagans

"While I was back in Tarsus, Barnabas came to seek me out and brought me with him to Antioch of Syria. After the martyrdom of Stephen and the persecution I had initiated, before I encountered the risen Christ, many followers of The Way that fled Jerusalem went to Antioch, but also traveled as far as to Phoenicia and Cyprus. They preached Jesus, but only did so among the Jews in those places. Ultimately, some believers from Cyprus and Cyrenia, after coming to Antioch, also preached Jesus to non-Hebrew people of the Greek culture who were neither Jews nor proselytes, that is Gentile people who had followed the

Jewish faith inasmuch as it focused on the Law of Moses and of sacrifices for sin.

"When the church in Jerusalem heard of these things their leadership sent Barnabas to Antioch. Many people were added to the church in Antioch under the leadership of Barnabas. Barnabas then went to Tarsus and brought me back to Antioch with him to join him in teaching the growing church in Antioch. It was there that people began to refer to believers in The Way as little Christs or Christians.

"I labored with Barnabas in Antioch for a year when prophets from Jerusalem came to Antioch and prophesied that a great famine was about to strike the whole world. That famine came during the reign of Claudius Caesar, who became emperor after Caligula, the great nephew of Tiberius. The believers in Antioch, both Jews and former pagans, decided to take up a collection to send to fellow believers in Jerusalem by way of Barnabas and myself. In a way, it was a peace offering to show that the believers were one, whether Jews that were of The Way or former pagans who now believed in Christ.

"Jerusalem was still primarily a church of those that were born Jews and now recognized Jesus Christ as the risen Messiah. Nevertheless, Jesus, before He ascended into heaven, commanded the disciples to go into the whole world from Jerusalem to Samaria and beyond to the ends of the earth teaching all peoples and making disciples and having them observe the things Jesus Himself taught.

"This started in Jerusalem on the day of Pentecost when the Holy Spirit came upon those waiting in an upper room as instructed by Jesus to wait for the coming of the Spirit. Subsequently, Philip, one of the deacons appointed together with Stephen, went down to Samaria, after the martyrdom of Stephen, when many scattered from Jerusalem to avoid persecution. Philip preached Christ to the Samaritans, and many believed.

"When the church in Jerusalem heard about it, they sent Peter and John to Samaria. There, when Peter and John came, the new Samaritan believers, who had been baptized by Philip in the name of Jesus, asked that they too might receive the Holy Ghost. So, Peter and John prayed for them to receive the Holy Ghost as they themselves had on Pentecost.

When they then laid their hands on them, the Samaritan believers received the Holy Ghost just as those of the Jewish church in Jerusalem had experienced.

"In addition, God had also sent Peter to a devout Roman Centurion named Cornelius whom God was also dealing with. Peter went to Cornelius with a delegation of Jewish believers from Joppa where Peter had been staying temporarily, to Caesarea, where Cornelius was based. Peter acknowledged, upon arrival, that he was breaking the traditions of the elders in coming to Cornelius and entering under his roof. However, Peter made it clear he was obeying the vision God had given him and that he could not make a distinction any longer with other people because they were not born Jews.

"Before Peter could even finish preaching Christ to Cornelius and his household, the Holy Ghost fell on them and all of them spoke in tongues, as the disciples first did on Pentecost. When he returned to Jerusalem, Peter was initially challenged by Jewish believers who rebuked Peter for even setting foot in the house of a Gentile. But after Peter rehearsed how God had led him and poured out the Holy Ghost on Cornelius and his household, those questioning Peter accepted the realization that salvation was not restricted to the Jews that believed on Jesus.

"Still, some Jewish believers, although accepting that salvation was available to former pagans that have come to accept Christ Jesus, believed that such new believers had to also adhere to all of the Jewish traditions. So, when Barnabas and I, along with Titus, a Gentile believer, went to Jerusalem with the gift from the believers in Antioch, this issue came up. James, Peter, and John, who were the pillars of the church in Jerusalem, gave their approval to the message I was preaching among the pagans. They sealed it by extending their hands in fellowship to me and Barnabas to go back to Antioch and continue preaching salvation, to even the pagans, through faith in the person and work of Jesus Christ and by God's grace."

A Jewish Church and a Gentile Church on Two Different Tracks

"The apostles also affirmed that belief in Jesus Christ was sufficient, and that it was unnecessary for believers who came out of their pagan backgrounds to observe Jewish traditions. Moreover, our companion Titus, who wasn't a Jew, was not compelled by them to be circumcised according to the Jewish tradition that began with God's instruction to Abraham.

"It was agreed that Barnabas and I should minister among the pagans, as God had anointed us to do, and that Peter and the others would continue teaching and preaching the good news of salvation through Jesus Christ to the Jews, as God had anointed them to do. Of course, that did not preclude me from preaching to my own Jewish brethren wherever I might find them, nor did that agreement preclude Peter and the other apostles from preaching to pagans, as indeed Peter had already done in the case of Cornelius the Centurion and which Peter, John, and Philip had done among the Samaritans. Before returning to Antioch, we brought John Mark, the cousin of Barnabas, along with us to help with the work in Antioch.

Scratching his curly head, Marcus said, "So Jesus is not just the God of the Jews?"

Paul responded, "God is the God of all and Lord of all. It is true that the knowledge of God came to the Jews first. Jesus was born to a virgin Jewish maiden, after she was overshadowed by the Holy Ghost. Her ancestry traced back to King David, as was the case with His earthly stepfather. Although the ministry of Jesus was among the Jews, it was the plan of God the Father that His Son should go first to the Jews. However, Jesus of Nazareth also intentionally went to the Samaritans, healed the child of a Syro-Phonecian woman, healed the servant of a Roman Centurion, and went to the predominantly Gentile region of the Gadarenes to deliver a man possessed of devils.

"From the beginning, God told Abraham, the father of our nation, that all nations would be blessed through him. Moreover, the prophet Isaiah reported that God, speaking of the Messiah, said, 'It is too small of a thing that You should be My Servant to raise up the tribes of Jacob, and to restore the preserved ones of Israel. I will also give You as a light to the Gentiles, that You should be My Salvation to the ends of the earth.'

"God's children, upon whom He pours out the riches of His grace, are not just Jews. And not all that are born as Jews are included. The prophet Hosea, speaking as the messenger of God, said, 'I will call them

My people which were not My people.' And he added, 'And it shall come to be, that in the place where it was said to them, you are not My people; there shall they be called the children of the living God.'

"It is not by keeping the Law of Moses or the traditions of the Jewish elders that a person is made right with God, but by believing on God's Son Jesus, whom He sent. It is by faith in Jesus that all people are made right with God. Even so, I have earnestly endeavored to preach Christ, first to my Jewish brethren, not wishing that any of them should be lost."

"Please explain God, His Son Jesus, and this Holy Ghost or Holy Spirit you keep talking about," asked Marcus.

Paul responded, "Our God is one and exists as the Godhead where these three manifestations of the Godhead reside as one and are co-equally God. The Godhead has always existed and is eternal. Apart from Him there is no God."

CHAPTER 6

From a Position of Safety to Boldly Carrying the Message of Salvation,
Through Jesus Christ, to Unreached Regions at Great Peril

"Antioch was a large city and a comfortable place to minister. It was also quite cosmopolitan with the influx of Jews that fled Jerusalem and of those from Cyprus and the northern coasts of Africa. There were several of us in the leadership of that church, besides me and Barnabas, that were prophets. This included two from Africa. While we were worshiping and fasting the Holy Spirit said through one, 'Separate out Paul and Barnabas for the work I have called them to do.' When they had fasted and prayed, they laid hands on us to commission us and sent us on our way."

"So, people become oracles of God by the Holy Spirit?" asked Marcus. "Indeed, this ability and other gifts are available to believers through the operation of the Holy Spirit," Paul responded.

The Mission Begins and Traditional Jews
Ramp Up Their Rejection of Jesus Christ

"Our initial stop was on the island of Cyprus, where Barnabas had been born. John Mark accompanied us that far. Beginning at Salamis we preached in the Jewish synagogues from there through the island to Paphos. There, the deputy of the country, Sergius Paulus, desired to hear our message and sent for Barnabas and me to speak with him. However, a Jewish sorcerer withstood us, not willing to lose his control of the deputy. Being moved by the Spirit, I confronted the sorcerer and condemned him to blindness for a season. When the deputy saw this, he believed our message.

"We then sailed from Paphos to the province of Pamphylia in Asia and went on to Perga, the capital city. In the meantime, John Mark chose to return to Jerusalem instead of accompanying us beyond Cyprus. After Perga, we went on to Pisidian Antioch and spoke in the synagogue there on the Sabbath once the leaders of the synagogue gave us the opportunity to speak. I addressed Jews and God-fearing non-Jewish proselytes among them. Outside were curious Gentiles who listened in to what I had to say. Beginning with the patriarchs, I preached Christ Jesus to them and the good news of salvation in His name.

"Afterwards, some of the Jews and proselytes followed us from the synagogue. But, outside, a crowd of pagan Gentiles asked that we speak to them on the following Sabbath. When the time came, it seemed like the whole city had come out to hear us.

"The rejectionist traditional Jews that remained with the synagogue were jealous when they saw the crowd and tried to dispute with us and, in the process, blasphemed. So, I quoted from the prophet Isaiah where God said of the Messiah to come, whom we preached was Jesus, that He had set Him to be a light to the Gentiles and for salvation to the ends of the world. I told the Jews that were opposing us that since they were unworthy and rejected our message, we would turn to the Gentiles.

"The Gentiles of that city rejoiced at our words. Many believed, and the word of the Lord spread through the region. However, the Jews that rejected our message stirred up a coalition against us including the rulers of that city. As a result, we were persecuted and put out of Pisidian Antioch. Shaking the dust of that city off us, we went on to Iconium.

"In Iconium, we went to the Jewish synagogue and preached the message of salvation through Jesus Christ. Many Jews and non-Jews received our message and we continued there for a while. However, the Jews that rejected our message worked with other Gentiles to stir them up against us, which divided the city. Those rejectionist Jews plotted with Gentiles to stone us to death. Therefore, we departed from Iconium and went on to the cities of Lystra and Derbe in the region of Lycaonia.

"While preaching in Lystra, I noticed a man nearby who was crippled in his feet from birth. Seeing that he had faith to be healed, I commanded him to stand up and walk. Immediately, the man that was lame got up and started leaping for joy. Those standing by began to proclaim that the gods had come down to them. Before we knew it the priest of Jupiter came with oxen to do sacrifice to us. Rending our garments and pleading with them that we were men just as they were, and that God wanted them to turn from such things to the living God. We barely were able to stop them from sacrificing to us as gods."

The Stoning of Paul

"Sometime later some rejectionist traditional Jews from Antioch and Iconium came to Lystra and stirred up the people against us so that they stoned me, dragged me to the outskirts of the city, and left me for dead. They had set upon me with intense rage. At the midpoint of the stoning, my spirit left my body. In my spirit I hovered over the scene as they continued to stone my lifeless body. I then followed them, in my spirit body, as they dragged my physical body on the road and dumped it outside the city as one would dump trash. At that time, I saw the Lord and I longed to go with Him and remain with Him. He said, 'Not now, Paul My son. I have much yet for you to do. You will testify of Me before rulers, including before Caesar.' As the disciples gathered about me, they mourned greatly, but no one had the faith or daring to speak life to me.

"The Holy Spirit raised me up with the same resurrection power that raised Jesus from the dead after three days and nights. My spirit re-entered my physical body and I stood up on my own. The disciples were astounded. Whereas they had thought they had to make plans to bury me, I, instead, walked with them back into Lystra. They didn't even have to carry me on a litter or put me on someone's back. I was greatly bloodied, and looked horrible from the ordeal, but I was as strong as any of them as we walked back into Lystra.

"As we walked back to Lystra, I recalled the stoning of Stephen and how God raised him up to pray that his persecutors would not be charged for his death. In a way, I felt that I had repaid a debt I owed

Stephen by enduring my own stoning. Yet, I knew from what the Holy Spirit had revealed to me in the deserts of the Arabian Kingdom of the Nabateans that there were other hardships I was destined to endure for Christ.

"That night, as the believers washed my wounds and gave me something to eat, they praised God for this great miracle of deliverance and were strengthened in their faith. A noble woman of the city, from a wealthy family, took a basin of water and knelt before me to wash my feet, a courtesy normally carried out by a servant. When a household servant rushed over to take her place, she kindly but firmly waved the servant away. She was determined not to be robbed of providing this service herself. Another woman of modest means, as could be ascertained from her faded, frayed, and mended garments, was one of the female Gentiles that had come to believe in Jesus through our preaching. She not only washed my many wounds, but she then kissed each bruise. I did not cry from the pain as I was being stoned, but her act of love and kindness brought tears from me as I recalled how my mother would kiss my little scrapes and bruises when I was a child. I blessed both women for their kindness and humility in attending to my needs. The next day Barnabas and I went to Derbe. Again, there was no soreness in my body from the stoning I had endured, nor was there any dizziness on my part from the terrible blows I had received to my head the day before."

"That was a miracle!" exclaimed Marcus.

"Indeed it was, Marcus, and a notable one at that! We preached Jesus in Derbe, then, assaying to return to Antioch, I established elders to lead the churches we had set up. On our return trip we again went to Lystra, Iconium, and Pisidian Antioch. Traveling through Pisidia we returned through the province of Pamphylia to Perga. After preaching again in Perga, we went down to the port city of Attalia where we took passage back to Syrian Antioch from where we had been sent out.

"Once back in Antioch, we reported on all the good news of our journey and how God had opened the door for Gentiles to believe and receive salvation. We then continued there at Antioch for a while."

CHAPTER 7

From Distinctions Based on Race, Class, and Gender to Oneness in Jesus Christ

"Peter came to Antioch from Jerusalem and mingled freely with the Gentile believers of the Antioch church, including partaking in meals with them. However, when James sent up a delegation from Jerusalem to see what was going on in Antioch, Peter broke away from eating with the Gentile believers. In the process, all the Jewish Christians did likewise so much so that even Barnabas got caught up in this and did the same.

"I confronted Peter face to face in front of them all. I said, 'How is it that you, a Jew, live like a Gentile, but then want to compel Gentile believers to live according to the practices of the Jews? Whether Jew or Gentile, we are all saved by faith in Christ and not by the works of the Law of Moses. No one is saved by the law, because all are guilty under the law since no one keeps it.' I made it clear that I am dead to the law but alive to God. I professed that I am crucified with Christ, but nevertheless, I am alive; yet it is not me that is living, but Christ is living in me by the Holy Spirit, and the life which I now live in the flesh I live by the faith of the Son of God, who loved me, and gave himself for me. I don't work against the grace God has given. If we are made right with God through the Law of Moses, then the sacrifice of Christ was unnecessary."

Christian Judaizers Pervert the Gospel and Cause Confusion

"In time, I got word from the churches we set up in Galatia that Judaizers, that is Christian Jews who nevertheless taught that the new non-Hebrew Christian believers had to keep all of the laws, customs, and teachings of the elders, had come into the churches saying I wasn't an apostle. These uninvited Judaizers perverted the message of the good news that we preached among the Galatians.

"Angered by what was happening in my absence, I wrote to those churches. I defended my apostleship and the message I preached of salvation by faith and belief in Jesus Christ, and the grace he made available to those who believe.

"I said I was an apostle, not by selection through casting lots or by the appointment of men, but by Jesus Christ, who Himself called me to be His apostle, and by God the Father, who raised Jesus up from the dead. I recalled that when I first met James, Peter, and John in Jerusalem, they seemed to be pillars in that church. They recognized the grace that was given to me to be an apostle to non-Hebrews. Therefore, they gave me and Barnabas their approval and made clear by their actions that they accepted that we should be messengers to non-Hebrews while they would be messengers to the Jews.

"I reproved the Galatians for departing so quickly from the true message of the gospel. I called down a curse on anyone that would trouble them with a perverted gospel that was different from what I had taught them. Besides, I didn't get that gospel from any human being, rather I received it by revelation from Jesus Christ. I made it clear that no one is saved by works according to the Law of Moses. I also emphatically wrote that, in Jesus Christ, there are not Jews on one hand and those not born Jews on the other hand. Likewise, there is no distinction between those that are slaves and those that are free. Further, there is no difference before God between males and females, rather we are all one in Christ Jesus.

"What I stood for was true, but was not easy for some to accept, because it turned everything they knew and had lived by upside down. Thus, Judaizers continued to try and undo the work the Holy Spirit had anointed me to do.

"Subsequently, men from Judea came up to Antioch in the province of Syria and taught that salvation was not possible without being circumcised and observing the Law of Moses. Thus, they frustrated the grace of God and offered a so-called salvation other than the sufficiency of the blood of Jesus. Barnabas and I disputed with them, but these Judaizers remained a problem and caused confusion among the Gentiles who believed in Jesus Christ.

"The church at Antioch sent me and Barnabas to Jerusalem to clear up this situation and make it plain, by the doctrine of the apostles, that Gentiles are saved by the grace of Jesus Christ and are not obligated by the Law of Moses or the traditions of the Jewish elders. On the way to Jerusalem from Antioch, Barnabas and I, as we journeyed through Phoenicia and Samaria, preached the gospel of Jesus Christ and of salvation by belief in Him and by His grace also to the Gentiles without the burden of Jewish laws and traditions. Our message was joyfully received, primarily because there was no barrier to their salvation if they turned from sin and believed on Jesus Christ, but also because they did not have to entirely turn their backs on their nation to adopt all the rules and ways of life of the Jews."

One Gospel Reaffirmed for both Jews and Gentile Believers

"When we got to Jerusalem, we were warmly received by the apostles, the elders, and the church. We gave account of our mission to Cyprus and through Galatia. But some in Jerusalem found it hard to leave the old way and insisted that Gentile believers had to submit to circumcision and keep the Law of Moses.

"But Peter stood up and reminded them how God had chosen him to go to Gentiles at Caesarea who received the message of salvation by grace, and that God demonstrated His approval by giving them the gift of the Holy Ghost just like they had received this gift. Peter wound up by saying, 'We Jews are saved by the grace of Jesus Christ just like the Gentiles are saved by that same grace.'

"Then Barnabas and I gave a full account of how God had brought salvation to the Gentiles through our preaching on our mission and confirmed it with many miracles and wonders.

"James then stood up to affirm that what Peter had done among Gentiles was in line with the words of the prophets. He proposed that they should not impose burdens on the Gentiles that believe but recommended sending some of their number from the church in Jerusalem to Antioch and through Syria and Cilicia with letters from the apostles at Jerusalem requiring only that they abstain from eating meat offered to idols, from fornication, from eating animals killed by strangulation, and from consuming the blood of animals. These messengers included John Mark, a close protégé of Peter, and Silas among them. So, Barnabas and I returned to the church in Antioch with these messengers and the letters from the apostles."

CHAPTER 8

From Pagan Idol Worshippers to Christians

"As Barnabas and I planned a return trip to Asia, to revisit the churches we had established, we had a hot disagreement as to whether John Mark should accompany us. John Mark was the cousin of Barnabas and had been with Peter, but I, recalling how he did not complete the last mission with us, did not want to take him with us this time. Therefore, my partnership with Barnabas was broken. Barnabas took John Mark with him to Cyprus, while Silas joined me."

A New Team Forms

"Since Barnabas and John Mark sailed to Cyprus, Silas and I headed out overland through Syria and Cilicia. When I returned to Derbe and Lystra, this time with Silas, we met Timothy, a believer whose mother was a Jewess, but his father was a Greek. Timothy was favorably known to the disciples in Lystra and Iconium. He became like a son to me. Because of the Jews in that area, who knew that his father was Greek, I circumcised Timothy myself. From that point, Timothy joined with us on our mission.

"As we went through the cities, we delivered to the churches the determination of the apostles at Jerusalem together with the limited number of rules they wanted them to abide by. The churches grew. After going about through Phyrigia and the region of Galatia, we looked about to determine what new region we should go to preaching Jesus Christ and that salvation had come to the Gentiles without the burden of Jewish religious laws and traditions. However, the Holy Spirit would not allow us to go into the province of Asia. So, we went to the region of Mysia and from there thought to go to north to the province of Bythinia, but the Holy Spirit blocked that too. We went through Mysia on to Troas. In Troas, we met Luke, whom you have met here Marcus. Luke then joined our party.

"Paul," asked Marcus, "when you say the Holy Spirit blocked options for you, what do you mean? How did that happen?"

"Marcus, the Holy Spirit communicates in different ways. In these instances, we did not have His peace. That is how we were blocked from going to places we thought would be good but were not God's will or timing for us just then.

"In Troas, I had a vision from God of a man from Macedonia bidding me to come over there and help them. We determined that was the will of God and sailed from Troas to the island of Samothracia and from there to the port of Neapolis in Macedonia. From Neapolis we journeyed up to Philippi. Philippi was the principal city of that region and was a city that had become a Roman colony where Roman army veterans were given certain rights to encourage them to take root there.

"After being in Philippi a few days, we went out of the city to a place on the river where people would habitually go to pray. There we spoke to the women. A certain businesswoman from Thyatira named Lydia heard us, believed, and was baptized, both she and all her household. She was our first convert in Europe. Lydia then constrained us to lodge in her home.

"We spent many days based in the home of Lydia, but when we went out and about, a girl possessed with a spirit of divination followed us proclaiming 'These men are the servants of the Most High God, and they show us the way of salvation.'

"The girl's masters got rich from the girl as people came to her as though she were an oracle and paid her owners for her revelations. I finally had enough and, turning toward her, commanded the spirit of divination to come out of her in the name of Jesus Christ."

Beaten for the Cause of Christ, but not Defeated

"When her masters saw that the source of their income was gone, they carried us off to the town center and stirred up the local authorities against us saying we were Jews and were troubling the city by teaching customs that were unlawful for Romans. Without a trial or questions, the local magistrates ripped off our clothes, had us beaten with rods, and thrown into prison.

"At midnight, Silas and I sang unto the Lord and praised Him. All of the prisoners heard us. Suddenly, there was an earthquake and our shackles and chains fell off and the prison doors sprang open. The same happened to the other prisoners.

"When the jailer realized what happened he sprang into the dark prison with a lamp. Realizing his life would be forfeit if the prisoners escaped, he drew his sword to take his own life. But I called out for him not to harm himself because we were all there. Falling to his knees, the jailer implored, 'Sirs, what do I have to do to be saved?' We answered that he should believe on the Lord Jesus Christ, and he would be saved as well as everyone in his household. The jailer then took us to his home where we preached Jesus to them. They all believed, so we took them out and baptized them. Afterwards, the jailer rejoiced, setting a meal before us and washed our wounds from the flogging at the hands of the local magistrates.

"In the morning, the magistrates sent word to release us and tell us to leave town. The jailer conveyed this news to us, but I was indignant. I said, 'We are Roman citizens. They had us publicly beaten without being condemned and now they want to have us go on our way quietly? No! Let the magistrates come here themselves and fetch us out.'

"When the sergeants of the magistrates relayed my demand, the magistrates feared reprisals and loss of position when they learned we were Romans. Coming to the prison, the magistrates walked us out and asked us to leave the city. We went back to Lydia's house and comforted the believers there before departing that city and continuing our journey."

CHAPTER 9

From Caesar Worship and Idol Gods to Jesus Christ the Son of God

"We journeyed on to Thessalonica passing through Amphipolis and Apollonia along the way. In Thessalonica, we went to a Jewish synagogue for three successive Sabbaths and preached Christ from the scriptures proclaiming that Jesus was the Christ. Some of the Jews of the synagogue were convinced and followed us. There was also a huge multitude of God-fearing Greeks and a good number of the chief women of the city that gathered to us.

"The rejectionist traditional Jews of the synagogue that determined not to believe that Jesus was the Messiah, but to keep with the old system of the Law of Moses, were greatly envious when they saw the large crowds of Greeks that believed and followed us. They hired some thugs to stir up the city against us and surrounded the house of Jason, where we had been lodging. They demanded that we be delivered over to them, but when they discovered that we were not there they drew out, by force, Jason and some of the brothers with him instead."

Turning the World Upside Down, Rejecting the Imperial Cult of Caesar Worship, and Demolishing Old Belief Systems

"Going to the chief officials of the city, they charged that Jason was harboring us, whom they described as those who were turning the world upside down and were now in Thessalonica to do the same. The mob accused us of doing things that were contrary to the decrees of Caesar and that we had proclaimed Jesus as king instead of Caesar. Once the rulers took charge of Jason and the brothers that were with him, they released them.

"Now Julius Caesar, Augustus Caesar, and Claudius Caesar all were declared to be divine and sons of a god. Julius Caesar was the first Caesar to accept worship as a god while he was still living. After his death, Julius Caesar was deified by the Roman state as divus, meaning in Latin that he became a god. Augustus Caesar was the first Roman emperor. Although he did not refer to himself as a god in Rome, being mindful how his adopted father Julius brought on his assassination in the senate by exalting himself, Augustus did allow the culturally Greek cities of the province of Asia and nearby provinces to build temples and altars to him. It was common for altars to Caesar Augustus to bear the inscription Caesar Divi Filius, meaning Caesar, son of god. That was the first manifestation of the Imperial Cult of the emperors.

"Tiberius Caesar did not have a male heir. Before he died, he adopted Germanicus' son Gaius, also known as Caligula. The leader of the Praetorian guard proclaimed Caligula as Princeps, or the first citizen, after the death of Tiberius. The Senate then ratified that choice. Caligula went on to build a temple to his own divinity. He also had his statues placed in Jewish synagogues in Alexandria, Egypt to receive cult or worship showing he was a god. Later, Caesar Caligula demanded that his statue also be installed in the Jewish Temple in Jerusalem.

"Caligula Caesar sent an army of more than three legions to Jerusalem, by way of Syria, to place his images in the Temple in Jerusalem by force, with orders to exterminate resisters and take all the rest as captives. However, before Petronius, his general entrusted with this mission, dared carry out his commands, Caligula was assassinated by an officer of the Pretorian guard. That ended the threat to set up Caesar's image in the Temple in Jerusalem to be worshipped.

"Claudius, who was the uncle of Caligula, then became Caesar. The Pretorian guard put forward Claudius, the younger brother of Germanicus, after taking him hostage and extracting a large bribe to each of the Praetorians.

"It was Claudius Caesar that expelled Jews from Rome, having wearied of the strife between the rejectionist traditional Jews and the Jewish Christians over whether Jesus Christ was indeed the Messiah and the Son of God, rendering sacrifices under the Mosaic system unnecessary following His sacrifice once for all who believe. Moreover, none of the Jews, whether members of the rejectionist traditional synagogues or the Christian Jews and the Gentiles that believed with them, would acknowledge the Caesars as divine or burn incense to them to show their loyalty to Caesar. The Caesars allowed the diverse people in the empire to keep their gods, and indeed imported some of those gods to Rome, such as Mithras from Persia, Diana from Ephesus, and Isis from Egypt, but they used the idea that Caesar was also a god to unify the disparate parts of the empire. The Jews, for a long time, believed an exception was carved out for them. In Jerusalem, they offered prayers and sacrifices for Caesar, to show loyalty, but did not sacrifice to Caesar or install his image in the Temple. Such was their compromise that Rome had accepted until Caesar Caligula attempted to impose his will on the Jews.

"As Caesar, Claudius defeated the Britons and added the province of Britannica to the empire. To celebrate his victory, he changed the name of his son to Britannicus. Claudius had four wives serially, the last being his niece, Agrippina. Agrippina got Claudius Caesar to adopt her son Nero, and name Nero as his successor over his own son Britannicus. Then Agrippina eventually poisoned Claudius so that her teenaged son Nero could become Caesar. After his death, Claudius was deified as a god by the Senate.

"The young Nero Caesar eventually had his mother murdered since she was trying to rule from behind the scenes. He also had his brother Britannicus killed to prevent any competition for the throne. In the meantime, Nero would imitate the sun god Sol, and had a huge sixty-cubit high bronze statue made of himself as the sun god outside the entrance to his huge palace, the Domus Aurea constructed after the great fire in Rome."

Departing Macedonia

"The brethren in Thessalonica sent us away by night to Berea. Gaius and Aristarchus of Macedonia joined our party as we continued our mission. At Berea, as was our custom, we went to the Jewish synagogue and preached Jesus Christ. The Jews at Berea were a noble sort that studied the scriptures to see if the things we said were true. Many of them believed together with many Greek men and notable Greek women. When the rejectionist traditional Jews of Thessalonica heard of it, they came down to Berea to stir up the people against us.

"The brethren in Berea escorted me to Athens while Silas and Timothy remained behind. However, after I arrived in Athens in the province of Achaia, I sent word for Silas and Timothy to join me immediately."

Evangelizing the Province of Achaia, Home of the Cultured Greeks

"While I waited for Silas and Timothy to join me in Athens, my spirit was troubled by the fact that the city was wholly given over to idolatry, worshiping all manner of idols. I spoke in the synagogue and the marketplace. Then certain philosophers of the stoics and epicureans brought me to the Areopagus below the Parthenon temple of many gods located on a high place. The philosophy of the stoics originated in Greece. They believe in living a life of virtue and to not complain at hardships. The philosophy of the epicureans also originated in Greece. They sought pleasure and wished to avoid pain.

"Both the stoics and epicureans wanted to hear this new thing I was preaching. I stood on the hill dedicated to Mars, their god of war, and said, 'You people of Athens are too superstitious. I have looked around and found altars to many different gods. I saw one altar to the Unknown God. It is Him that I wish to declare to you.'

"I preached that we are all God's offspring and ought not to think that the Godhead is like an image of gold, silver, or stone, formed by the hand of man. I also preached that Jesus Christ rose from the dead and will raise us up from the dead too. Upon hearing of the resurrection from the dead, some mocked me, but others clung to me and would hear me again.

Among those that believed were Dionysius the Areopagite, a woman named Damaris, and others along with them."

An Expanded Team Includes Women as Leaders

"From Athens I went on to Corinth. In Corinth I met Aquila, a man from the province of Pontus on the Black Sea, and his wife Priscilla. They were Jews that came to Corinth from Rome when Claudius Caesar expelled all Jews from Rome. Being of the same trade, I dwelt with them and worked alongside them as a tentmaker.

"I found time there to write to the believers in Rome. I let them know that they were regularly in my prayers and that I had been seeking an opportunity to go to Rome and preach among them. I wrote that God had made it possible for all people to know Him, but people rejected Him and instead worshiped beasts, birds, and insects. Since they rejected the true God, God gave them over to their vile appetites, wherein they chose to do all sorts of things against decency and nature.

"I made it plain that, although Jews are chosen by God as a special people, whether Jew or non-Jew, all have sinned coming short of God's glory and are condemned by the law. However, justification is freely available by the grace of God through the redemption that is in Christ Jesus. It is this Jesus that God provided as an acceptable offering to pay the penalty of sin, through faith in Him and His blood. This righteousness that He makes available removes all past sin, through the plan of God wherein He judges sin but justifies those that believe in Jesus.

"God is not just the God of the Jews, but also of non-Jews. This one God justifies the Jews that are under the covenant of circumcision and the non-Jews who are not under that covenant of circumcision. Both are made just by faith in Jesus Christ, the Son of God, who paid the penalty of sin for all who accept who He is and what He did, by faith."

Justification by Faith

"Abraham believed God while he was yet uncircumcised and is the father of all who believe. His belief was imputed to him as righteousness.

Therefore we, whether Jew or non-Jew, are justified by faith and we have peace with God through the Lord Jesus Christ.

"God showed His love for us by sending His Son to die for the ungodly while we were still His enemies. We are justified by the blood of Jesus and by His sacrifice we are reconciled to God. As Jesus died for our sins and was raised again to life, we must consider ourselves dead to sin but alive to God in Christ. Therefore, we no longer allow ourselves to become instruments of unrighteousness for the purposes of sinning, but we turn ourselves over to God, as people made alive from the dead, and our members are become instruments of righteousness devoted to God. The price of sin is death, but God gives us the gift of eternal life through our Lord Jesus Christ.

"This means that those who are in Christ Jesus and walk not according to the flesh, but to the Spirit, are free from condemnation. Those that are living according to the flesh cannot please God, because to be fleshly minded is death. But you are not in the flesh, but in the Spirit, if the Spirit of God dwells in you. If the Spirit of He that raised up Jesus from the dead dwells in you, the one that raised Christ from the dead will also quicken your mortal bodies by His Spirit that is now living in you.

"If we choose to live according to the flesh, we will die, but if we, through the Spirit, put to death the deeds of the body, we will live. For as many as are led by the Spirit of God, are sons of God. We have received the Spirit of adoption, so we have the right to cry out, Papa, Father! The Spirit Himself bears witness to our spirits that we are God's children. If we are children, then we are heirs, heirs of God, and joint heirs with Christ.

"What then can separate us from the love of Christ, tribulation, distress, persecution, famine, nakedness, peril, or execution? It is written, For Your sake we are killed all day long; we are considered to be like sheep to be slaughtered. No, in all these things we are more than conquerors through Him that loved us.

"I am persuaded that neither death, nor life, nor angels, nor principalities, nor powers, nor things present, nor things to come, nor height, nor depth, nor any other creature shall be able to separate us from the love of God, which is in Christ Jesus our Lord.

"Concerning how one attains salvation, I said, the word is very nearby, even in your mouths, and in your hearts: that is to say the word of faith, which we preach. What we preach is this: If you confess with your mouth that Jesus Christ is Lord and believe in your heart that God raised Him from the dead, you will be saved. It works this way; with the heart a man believes, and righteousness is imputed to him, and with his mouth confession that Jesus Christ is Lord is made resulting in salvation.

"Stop!" pleaded Marcus. "You mean by confessing the Lordship of Jesus Christ out loud, and truly believing in my heart what I have openly confessed, I am saved from my sins without the need of offering sacrifices of animals, vowing to do great deeds, or giving offerings of gold and silver?'

"Yes," said Paul. "You are not far from God's kingdom, Marcus, if you act on what you have just said. In this there is no difference between Jews and non-Jews: for the same Lord is over all and is rich to all that call on him. Whoever calls on the name of the Lord will be saved.

"Such were my words in the letter to the believers in Rome. I had been longing to go to Rome, but the opportunity had not yet presented itself. In the meantime, I went to the synagogue in Corinth every week and preached. "In time, Silas and Timothy rejoined me from Macedonia with a good report of what was going on in the Church in Thessalonica, but I felt it necessary to send Timothy back to Thessalonica in Macedonia. Silas went back with him. "I wrote a letter to the church in Thessalonica, signed by myself, Timothy, and Silvanus, to be delivered by Timothy. In my letter, I reminded the church at Thessalonica that our gospel was not just presented to them in word, but also in power, and in the Holy Ghost. We thanked God for them at Thessalonica because when they received the word of God which they heard from us, they received it, not as the word of men, but as the truth that it was, the word of God, which effectively works in those that believe.

"I called on them to abstain from fornication because God has called us to holiness, not uncleanness. I also sought to comfort them concerning the Lord's return that they should not be sorrowing over those among them that died as though they would miss out on the Lord's return.

"For the Lord Himself will descend from heaven with a shout, like the voice of an archangel, which is God's trumpet, and the dead in Christ will rise first, then we which are alive and remain at the Lord's coming will be caught up together with them in the clouds, to meet the Lord in the air: thus, shall we be with the Lord forever. However, His coming will be like a thief in the night, so we must stay ready. In that regard I called on them to pray continually, be open to the moving of the Holy Spirit, not despising prophetic utterances, but testing everything and accepting that which is good.

"At that time, I began to preach more earnestly in Corinth that Jesus is the Christ. When the rejectionist traditional Jews of the synagogue opposed me to the point of blaspheming, I shook the dust of that place from my clothes and said let your blood be on your own heads; I am clean and blameless: from now on I will go to the Gentiles.

"After that, I moved into the home of Justus, whose home was attached to the side of the synagogue. Crispus, the leader of the synagogue, believed, together with his whole household. I baptized him along with Stephanas, but Crispus was soon replaced by Sosthenes, as the head of the synagogue."

Jesus Appears Again to Encourage Paul

"After these happenings, I received a vision in the night. The Lord spoke to me in the vision and told me not to be afraid and to speak, not keeping silent, because He was with me, and He also had many people in Corinth; no one would harm me. Therefore, I continued preaching in Corinth for a year and a half.

"Upon again getting word from Thessalonica, I wrote another letter to the church at Thessalonica. I sought to put their hearts at ease concerning the timing of the Lord's return. I went into detail concerning signs, and those things that will happen prior to the Lord's return. Finally, I gave them sound wisdom regarding keeping peace and order in the church.

"When Gallio became the Roman proconsul of the province of Achaia, Sosthenes, the new leader of the synagogue, in a conspiracy with the rejectionist traditional Jews of the synagogue, brought a case against me to Gallio's judgement seat. They alleged that I was persuading men to worship God in ways that were contrary to traditional Jewish religious law. But before I could open my mouth in my own defense, Gallio spoke up to dismiss the case against me as being without merit under Roman law. Gallio then had Sosthenes thrown out of the judgment seat, which was followed by the Greeks giving Sosthenes a sound thrashing.

"Afterwards, I remained in Corinth a while longer before taking a ship to Syria with Priscilla and Aquila to accompany me. At that time, I shaved my head because I had taken a Nazarite vow in preparation for going to Jerusalem to keep one of the Jewish festivals.

"I left Pricilla and Aquila in Ephesus and reasoned with the Jews in Ephesus. They would have had me stay longer, but I declined. From Ephesus I sailed down to Caesarea, went on to Jerusalem for the festival and then traveled back to Antioch where I gave account to the church of those things that happened on this second mission. I then set out on a third mission going back over the churches set up in the regions of Galatia and Phrygia."

Clarifying the Gospel Message

"In the meantime, Apollos of Alexandria, Egypt came to Ephesus and preached mightily, but he only knew of John's baptism. Priscilla and Aquila pulled Apollos aside privately and explained the truth to him more clearly and fully. Not wishing to linger in Ephesus, Apollos went to Achaia, with letters of recommendation from the church in Ephesus before I could meet with him in Ephesus. In Achaia, Apollos preached to the Jews publicly convincing them from the scriptures that Jesus was the Christ.

"While Apollos was in Achaia, I finally made my way to Ephesus in the province of Asia. There I encountered a group of about a dozen disciples. When I asked if they had received the Holy Ghost since they believed, they replied that they didn't even know there was a Holy Ghost, but they had been baptized with the baptism of John. I told them that

John truly taught the baptism of repentance, but he also taught that they should believe on the one that would come after him, that is one Jesus Christ. When they heard and received this, they were baptized in the name of Jesus Christ. Once I then laid my hands on them, they all received the Holy Ghost and spoke in tongues."

Evangelist in Residence at the School of Tyrannus

"When I went into the synagogue, for about three months I preached Jesus Christ disputing with and persuading the traditional Jews. But when they hardened their hearts against my message and began to speak evil things against me before the crowds, I separated from them. Taking the disciples with me, I taught in the school of Tyrannus for two years, in which time everyone in the province of Asia, both Jews and Gentiles heard the message of Jesus Christ.

"During those two years in Ephesus, teaching in the school of Tyrannus, I wrote three letters to the church in Corinth. In my first letter to the church at Corinth, I wrote that they should not keep company with fornicators. Specifically, if a man says he is a believer, but is a fornicator, or is covetous of the things of others, or is an idolater, or is a brawler, or a drunkard, or an extortioner, they should not break bread with such a person, especially at the Lord's table.

"In my second letter to the church at Corinth, I pleaded that they be not divided into factions, but rather be of the same mind. I said this because I had learned from Chloe's household of contention. Some were saying I am a follower of Paul; or I am a follower of Apollos; or I am a follower of Peter; or I am a follower of Christ. I made it clear that Christ is not divided into factions. I wasn't crucified for them, and no one was baptized in my name. The only foundation is that of Jesus Christ.

"I also had to address a serious matter of fornication that was so bad that you didn't even hear anything like it mentioned among the heathen. That is to say that a man in the church was sleeping with his stepmother, his father's wife. I instructed them to put him out and not have fellowship with him.

"Regarding fornicators in general, I wrote that their bodies are part of the body of Christ. Therefore, if a person consorts with a prostitute, that person becomes one with the prostitute and joins that prostitute with Christ. May God forbid that this should be. Therefore, I wrote that they should flee fornication because their bodies are the temple of the Holy Ghost who is in them and given to them from God. They are not their own then to do as they please, but should glorify God in their bodies and spirits, which are God's.

"I gave instruction on the whole subject of marriage and the rules that apply within marriage. I then gave advice concerning eating meat sold in the market stalls that may have been offered to idols.

"Once again, I defended my status as an apostle, having seen Jesus and been given a ministry among Greeks and other non-Jews. I had all the liberty of an apostle even if I didn't demand the things that should come to an apostle, or marry and travel with a wife, as did Peter and other apostles.

Revelations from Jesus

"Although I wasn't present at the Lord's last supper, the Lord revealed to me everything as though I were there. It was from that revelation from the Lord Jesus Christ that I wrote instructions on how that supper is to be remembered and honored.

"I imparted understanding about spiritual gifts. Although there are different gifts, administrations of those gifts, and operations of those gifts, it is from one Spirit, and we are all part of the same body. More important than the various gifts is that we operate in love.

"In reviewing the gospel of Jesus Christ, which I preached among them with a focus on the death and resurrection of Jesus Christ, I clarified that we too shall be changed as resurrected beings putting off the flesh that is subject to corruption and putting on immortality.

"Finally, I gave instructions on setting aside a donation to the church in Jerusalem, as the churches in Macedonia had done."

Miracles and Confrontation in Ephesus as Worship of the Great Mother Goddess is Diminished

"God worked special miracles by my hands while I was in Ephesus. Ephesus was a great city and was a center of the worship of the goddess Diana, also known as Artemis. Strips of cloth that had been on my body were cut into pieces and laid on the bodies of the sick, and they were both healed and evil spirits departed from them.

"Now a certain group of Jewish men, seven sons of a Jewish priest named Sceva, went to the house of a man possessed by an evil spirit. They commanded the evil spirit, in the name of Jesus that I preached, to come out of the man. But the spirit spoke up saying, 'I know of Jesus, and I know of Paul, but who are you?' And with that the possessed man overpowered them all, thrashing them all soundly so that they fled the house naked and wounded. When word of this got out both Jews and Gentiles feared God and lifted high the name of Jesus.

"In those days many believed on Jesus Christ and came forth to publicly confess their sins. Many also that had books on the workings of the occult brought those books. We held a great bonfire to destroy those books whose value was of a great sum of money valued at fifty thousand pieces of silver. The word of God was honored, and the church grew.

"I sent Timothy and Erastus from Ephesus to Macedonia while I remained at Ephesus. No sooner had Timothy and Erastus departed than Demetrius, a silversmith, stirred up the city against me and The Way. Demetrius called together craftsmen of the same profession telling them, 'You know we have amassed great wealth from the worship of Diana and the selling of our images. Now you both see and hear that, not just in Ephesus, but almost throughout the province of Asia, this Paul has persuaded people to believe in The Way. In the process, he has turned many people away from the worship of Diana and other gods, saying a god made by human hands is not a god. The result is that our craft of making and selling images is about to come to nothing, but also, the temple of the great goddess Diana, who is worshipped throughout the province of Asia and indeed the whole world, is being despised, and her magnificence is in danger of being destroyed.'

"When the silversmith idol makers heard the words of Demetrius, they worked themselves into a frenzy and cried out, saying, 'Great is Diana of the Ephesians!' The whole city was stirred up but confused. They took Gaius and Aristarchus, two Macedonians that were my travel companions, and rushed into the great theater on the mountainside facing the harbor.

"The theater was the largest in the province of Asia and could accommodate over 25,000 people. It was being renovated and expanded as part of a project initiated by Claudius Caesar. I wanted to go into the theater and take them on, but the brothers would not permit me to do so. In addition, some members of the governor's staff, who were friends of mine, came to me and likewise asked that I not go into the theater during the tumult stirred up by Demetrius and the members of his craft who made their wealth from making and selling idols of Diana."

"Diana, also known as Artemis, of the Ephesians, was worshipped throughout the countries surrounding the Great Sea. Ephesus was the largest city in the world after Rome and the Temple of Diana in Ephesus was a notable monument, the largest temple in the world, and it attracted devotees from other countries of the world. The goddess was worshipped in other countries with different names, such as Cybele, Isis, Mithras, Ishtar, Inanna, Ashtaroth, and others, but was the same mother goddess around which a cult of veneration and sexuality was developed. Because the empire that is Rome encompasses many countries, these goddesses are worshiped in Rome by their native names.

An idol of Diana of the Ephesians at Ephesus, Archaeologists Recovered from being Buried in Sand and Mud, with the Author Standing Nearby to Demonstrate its Size.

"Now most of the people in the theater didn't know why they were there. The rejectionist traditional Jews assayed to put Alexander, a traditional Jew, forward to address the crowd and use the opportunity to speak against me and the message of Jesus Christ. But when it was realized that he was a Jew, the crowd chanted for about two hours saying, 'Great is Diana of the Ephesians!' Finally, the town clerk appeared and rebuked Demetrius and directed him to bring any charges to the proper venue. Warning the crowd that they could be charged with an unlawful assembly that would earn the ire of Rome, he was able to settle the crowd down and dismiss them."

The GREAT THEATER of EPHESUS

CHAPTER 10

From Witnessing to Individuals in Synagogues to Witnessing to the Masses, Rulers of Nations, and the World

"After the uproar in Ephesus had quieted down, I embraced the believers in Ephesus and headed out for Macedonia by way of Troas. While in Macedonia, I wrote a third letter to the church in Corinth and all the saints in Achaia. In that letter, I let them know of the perils Timothy and I had come through in the province of Asia and thanked them for their prayers. I let them know that we have this treasure of the light and life of the Holy Spirit in the earthen vessels of our mortal bodies, that the excellency of the power may attributed to God, and not to us.

"Concerning our tribulations, I wrote that we were troubled on every side, but not distressed; we were perplexed, but did not despair; persecuted, but not forsaken; cast down, but not destroyed. We went about bearing in our bodies the death of the Lord Jesus that the life of Jesus might also be manifest in our bodies. Though our outward man is perishing, yet our inward man is renewed day by day. We don't look at things that can be seen, but at the things which are not seen, for the things which are seen are temporal, but the things which are not seen are eternal.

"I explained that we walk by faith and not by sight. Our role is as ambassadors for Christ, as though God was beseeching them by us. So, we appealed to them on behalf of Christ that they choose to be reconciled to God. God made Jesus Christ, who knew no sin, to become sin for us that we might be made the righteousness of God in Him.

"My intention was to visit them from Macedonia and so I asked that they be prepared with their gift for the church in Jerusalem, especially if some of the Macedonians were to decide to accompany me to Achaia. But they should give freely and with a joyful heart. For God is able to make all grace abound toward them, that they, always having all sufficiency in all things, may abound to every good work.

"Though we walk in the flesh, we don't carry out our warfare by the flesh. Because the weapons we fight with are not flesh or made by human hands but are mighty through God to pull down strong holds. Therefore, I encouraged them to cast down imaginations, and every high thing that exalts itself against the knowledge of God and bring into captivity every thought to the obedience of Christ."

Paul's Defense of His Apostleship

"Once more I had to write to them about my credentials as an apostle because of those who, in my absence, spoke disparagingly of me and attempted to pervert the gospel I had preached among them. I described myself and my ministry as not one bit behind the very top apostles.

"False apostles, who were deceitful workers, made themselves out to be apostles of Christ. And no surprise, because Satan himself can make himself appear to be an angel of light. Therefore, it is not a big thing for his ministers to present themselves as ministers of righteousness, but their end will be according to their works.

"I presented my credentials, with their indulgence, understanding it might seem like boasting. I said, 'They want to glory in their flesh and deeds, well I can do so too. Are they Hebrews? So am I. Are they Israelites? So am I. Are they the seed of Abraham? So am I. Are they ministers of Christ? (I said this foolishly) I am more. My labors in Christ are more abundant, I have endured stripes from floggings above measure, I have been imprisoned more frequently, in peril of death often. Of the Jews five times I received forty stripes save one. Three times was I beaten with rods, once was I stoned, three times I suffered shipwreck, a night and a day I have been in the deep sea. I have journeyed, I have survived perils of waters, perils of robbers, perils by my own countrymen, perils by the heathen, perils in the city, perils in the wilderness, in perils in the sea, and in perils among false brethren. I have endured weariness and painfulness, I have often watched through the night in prayer, in hunger and thirst, fasting often, in cold and nakedness. Beside all those things I daily bear the care of all the churches. If I must glory, I will glory in my weaknesses.'

"In Damascus, the governor under King Aretas IV kept the city of the Damascenes with a garrison, intending to apprehend me, but I escaped his hands by being let down in a basket from a window in the city wall. Lest I become puffed up from the revelations given to me, I was given a thorn in the flesh. Three times I asked the Lord to remove it, but He said, 'My grace is sufficient for you, because My strength is made perfect in your weakness.' Therefore, I will most gladly glory in my weaknesses so that the power of Christ may rest upon me. Thus, I take pleasure in weakness, in reproaches, in necessities, in persecutions, and in distresses for Christ's sake: for when I am weak, then am I strong.

"While I was in Macedonia, I revisited the churches in Macedonia and then went down to the province of Achaia, again visiting those churches. When I prepared to sail from there back to Syria, I learned of another conspiracy by rejectionist traditional Jews to lay a trap for me in order to kill me. Therefore, I returned to Philippi in Macedonia and arranged to cross over into the province of Asia again. From Philippi I was accompanied into Asia by Sopater of Berea; Aristarchus and Secundus of Thessalonica; Gaius of Derbe in the province of Galatia, Timothy; and Tychicus and Trophimus of the province of Asia.

"Upon coming to Troas, we met with the believers there for a week. On the last night, I preached at length in a large building. Many saw lights flashing in the upper reaches of the chamber being angels that were in our midst. However, a young lad named Eutychus fell asleep from a high perch in a third level window and fell down. Those that took up his body pronounced him dead, but I rushed to him and taking him in my arms I said, 'Don't let yourselves be troubled because his life is in him.' I then went back to speaking through the night until dawn. I ate something and departed. The young man was taken home alive, which was a great comfort to all that were there."

Preparing Church Leaders to Carry On without Him

"I sent my companions by ship from Troas to Assos with instructions to wait for me there while I walked to Assos. From Assos we sailed along the coast to Mitylene. From Mitylene, we sailed in rapid succession to Chios, Samos, Trogyllium, and then to Miletus, bypassing Ephesus so as not to be delayed given my desire to get to Jerusalem before Pentecost. At Miletus, I sent for the elders of the church at Ephesus. When they arrived, I charged them anew with the care of the church and to be on guard for false brothers whom the Holy Ghost had shown me would try to come into the church. I made this my farewell speech recounting my ministry, advising them that in every place I had traveled recently, the Holy Ghost spoke through prophets about the chains and hard times that awaited me in Jerusalem.

"I made the elders and overseers of the church know that none of these things moved me, neither did I count my life something to be spared, so that I might finish my assignment with joy, and fulfill the ministry, which I received directly from the Lord Jesus, to testify of the gospel of the grace of God. I told them they would not see my face again. After I kneeled and prayed with them, they all hugged me and kissed my neck with tears and sorrow for the things I had told them and that they would not see me again.

"After the elders accompanied me to our ship, we took a straight course to Cos and Rhodes. From there we went to Patara and found a ship going to Phoenicia. We sailed past Cyprus and landed at Tyre. We stayed in Tyre for a week with fellow believers. These brothers, speaking by the Holy Ghost, said I should not go to Jerusalem. Our company left Tyre and went south to Ptolemais, where we spent a day with the believers there, and then went to Caesarea. At Caesarea we stayed in the home of Philip the evangelist, who was one of the seven original deacons of the church in Jerusalem. Philip had four daughters, all virgins, and all prophesied. While we spent a few days in Philip's house, Agabus, a prophet, came down from Judea and met us there.

"When Agabus approached, he took my belt and bound my hands and feet with it, and said, 'The Holy Ghost says, this is the way the Jews at Jerusalem will bind the man that owns this belt, and they will deliver him over to the Gentiles.'

"When those present heard these things from Agabus, both my companions and the believers in Caesarea pleaded with me not to go up to Jerusalem. I spoke to them asking, 'What do you mean by crying and breaking my heart?' I said, 'I am ready not just to be put in chains, but also to die at Jerusalem for the name of the Lord Jesus.'

"When they saw that I could not be persuaded otherwise, they said, 'Let the Lord's will be done.' We then went up to Jerusalem. Some of the believers in Caesarea went up with us including Mnason, an elderly believer from Cyprus who had a house in Jerusalem where we could stay."

Giving a Good Report at Jerusalem

"When we arrived in Jerusalem, we were warmly received by the believers there. On the following day we met with James, the brother of Jesus, and the elders of the church at Jerusalem. I reported to them on all the things the Lord had done among the Gentiles through my ministry. When they heard it they glorified God.

"I was then apprised of the thousands of Jews in Jerusalem that believed on the Lord Jesus Christ, but who were also zealous to keep the commandments of Moses. Because some had heard that I taught Jews that live among Gentiles not to observe the laws of Moses and the traditions of our ancestors, they warned that people would be watching me to see if this report were true. Although James said they did not want to put on the Gentile believers any obligation other than what the council in Jerusalem had previously decided and written by letters, he asked that I take a vow with four others, shave my head, and go to the temple to demonstrate that these reports were not true and that I too observe the Law of Moses.

"I then entered the Temple with these men for seven days of purification. At the completion of that purification, some rejectionist traditional Jews from the province of Asia who denied Jesus Christ had come down to the Temple and recognized me. They cried out, 'You men of Israel, help us!' Pointing me out they said, 'This is the man that is teaching all men everywhere against the Jewish people, the Law of Moses, and this Temple, and further he has brought Greeks into the

Temple and, in doing so, has polluted this holy place.' They said this because they had seen me in the city with Trophimus, an Ephesian, and presumed that I had brought him into the Temple.

"The whole city was thus in an uproar. My accusers had the mob drag me out of the Temple, the doors of the Temple grounds being shut behind me and commenced to try and beat me to death on the street. Word came to the commander of the Roman garrison in Jerusalem, and he rushed down with centurions and soldiers. Seeing this, the mob left off beating me and the commanding officer of the Roman garrison had me chained and taken into custody. When the commander demanded to know who I was and what I had done the mob cried out charges against me, but they contradicted themselves. Therefore, I was taken under guard to the castle, but the mob followed yelling, 'Kill him!'"

Paul's Defense Before the Mob

"Before entering the castle where the Roman soldiers were garrisoned, I asked the commanding officer if I could have a word with him. He was surprised that I spoke Greek and at first presumed that I was a notorious Egyptian brigand. I assured him that I, Paul, was a Jew of Tarsus, a major city in the province of Cilicia, and I besought him to allow me to address the people. He granted my request. When I stood on the stairs of the castle and raised my hand a great silence came over the crowd. Addressing them in Hebrew, they became even more attentive. The still silence with me standing above them and the castle wall behind me made it possible for all to hear my voice clearly. I proceeded to give my testimony and defense of the gospel.

"I said, 'I am truly a Jewish man. Although I was born in Tarsus, a city in the province of Cilicia, I was brought up in this city and studied at the feet of Gamaliel. I was taught according to the strict way of the law of our ancestors, and I was zealous regarding God, as I know all of you are here today. I persecuted The Way to the point of death, arresting and delivering both men and women into prisons. The high priest knows this quite well. He and the elders of the Sanhedrin can confirm that

I received from them letters to present to the leaders of synagogues beyond Jerusalem conveying on me the authority to search out followers of The Way and bring them bound in chains back to Jerusalem to receive punishment. I went with those letters to Damascus in Syria.

"It happened that, as I was approaching near to Damascus on my journey at about the noon hour, a great bright light from heaven shined around me. I was dazed and my horse was startled. Falling to the ground I heard a voice speaking to me saying, 'Saul, Saul, why are you persecuting me?' I responded, 'Who are you Lord?' And He said, 'I am Jesus of Nazareth, the one you are persecuting.' The men with me on my mission saw the light and were frightened, but they did not hear the voice of He that spoke with me. I said, 'What do You want me to do Lord?' The Lord, addressing me said, 'Get up. Go into Damascus and there you will be told all of the things that are determined for you to do.' I stood up, but I was blinded by that glorious light and could not see. Those from Jerusalem that were with me led me by hand into Damascus. "There in Damascus a man named Ananias, a devout man who lived according to the Law of Moses and who had a good reputation among the Jews living in Damascus, came to me. Standing before me, Ananias said, 'Saul my brother, receive your sight.' At that same moment I was able to see him. "Ananias went on to say, 'The God of our ancestors has chosen you to know His will, see the Righteous One, and hear His voice from His mouth because you will be His witness to all people of what you have seen and heard.' Ananias concluded saying, 'What are you waiting for? Get up and get baptized, washing away your sins, and calling on the name of the Lord.'

"When I eventually came to Jerusalem again, as I prayed in the Temple, I was in a trance. I saw the Lord saying to me, 'Hurry up and get out of Jerusalem as fast as you can because they won't receive your testimony concerning me.' I responded saying, 'Lord, they know that I beat and imprisoned from every synagogue those that believed on You. Also, when the blood of your martyr Stephen was shed, I stood by giving my consent to his death while I watched over the clothes of those that killed him.' But He said, 'Move out! I am sending you from here to the Gentiles.'

"They listened to me up until the moment I said 'Gentiles.' They then raised their voices again saying, 'He doesn't deserve to live, let's take him out from this world.' As they yelled and threw off their clothes to make it easier to throw stones and threw dust up in the air in their rage, the commanding officer of the Roman garrison ordered that I be brought into the castle and interrogated by flogging me in order to find out why the mob was so incensed against me.

"As the Roman soldiers hung me up from a beam by leather thongs tied around my arms and hands, I said to the centurion that was overseeing the beating that was about to take place, 'Is it in compliance with the law for you to flog a Roman citizen that has not been found guilty of an offense?'

"Upon hearing my question, the centurion went and told the commanding officer warning him, to be careful what he did with me because I was a Roman citizen. With that the commanding officer came and asked me, 'Tell me, are you really a Roman citizen?' I answered, 'Yes.' Then the commander said, 'I purchased this freedom with a great sum of money.' I responded, 'But I was born free.'

"Immediately, the interrogation detail took me down, removed the leather thongs they had bound me with and left the room.

"The commander was fearful, once he realized I was a Roman citizen, and because he had instructed that I be bound and hung up to be interrogated by flogging. The next day, in order to determine why the Jews were leveling accusations against me, he not only left me unfettered, but ordered the chief priests and the whole Sanhedrin to come to the castle. When they arrived, they approached no closer than the castle courtyard, because they dared not enter a place of Gentiles. The commander then had me stand before them.

"Looking on the gathering of the Sanhedrin and its officers, I began to speak saying, 'You men and my brothers, I have lived with a good conscious before God until this very day.' But before I could utter another word, Ananias, the high priest at that time, ordered one of the Sanhedrin's guards standing next to me to strike me on my mouth. With blood trickling down my split lip, I snapped back saying, 'God will strike you, you whitewashed grave wall! How can you sit in judgment of me according to the law, and yet you order me to be slapped contrary to the law?'

"The Sanhedrin's officers that stood around me were shocked. They closed in on me and said, 'How dare you rebuke God's high priest!' I responded, 'Brothers, I didn't know he was the high priest, because it is written that one should not speak disparagingly of the ruler of the people.'

"I looked around and could see by their dress that part of the Sanhedrin was Sadducee, and the other part was Pharisee. The Sadducees don't believe in the resurrection or in angels or spirits, while the Pharisees believe both. Then I lifted up my voice and cried out, 'Men and brothers, I am a Pharisee and the son of a Pharisee. It is because of the hope of the resurrection of the dead that I am being called into question.'

"My words divided the Sanhedrin and their officers and staff. A great tumult arose and the scribes that were identified with the Pharisee's position stood up and said, 'We don't find any problem with him. If a spirit or an angel spoke with him, let's not put ourselves in the position of fighting against God.' The Roman commanding officer, looking at this, was afraid I would be physically torn apart between the Sadducees and the Pharisees, so he commanded his soldiers to go down into the melee and to bring me by force back into the castle."

Jesus Appears to Paul Yet Again Reconfirming His Assignment to Witness of Him in Rome

"That night the Lord Jesus stood near me in my chamber in the castle and said, 'Cheer up, Paul. Just as you have testified of me here in Jerusalem, you must do the same also in Rome.' I was greatly encouraged by yet another visitation from the Lord."

A Conspiracy Between Assassins, the High Priests, and the Sanhedrin

"The following morning, about forty rejectionist traditional Jews who denied Jesus Christ bound themselves with a curse, saying they would neither eat nor drink until they had killed me. This group went to the high priests and other members of the Sanhedrin to reveal their vow.

They conspired with the Sanhedrin to have the Sanhedrin request of the Roman commanding officer that I be brought before them again the next morning, under the ruse of wanting to know more perfectly my position. This group of assassins would then use the opportunity to attack and kill me. However, my nephew, the son of my sister, heard their scheme and came to the castle to reveal the plot to me. Upon hearing this I called for one of the centurions and told him to take the lad to the commanding officer, because he had something to tell him.

"Once my nephew was brought to the commanding officer, he took him by the hand and pulled him aside to inquire privately about his message. My nephew revealed the conspiracy of the Jews against me and warned the commanding officer not to give in to this tactic because over forty assassins will be lying in wait for me, bound by an oath to neither eat nor drink until they have killed me. My nephew added, 'Now they are ready and are looking for you to promise to bring my uncle Paul to the Sanhedrin's court.'

"The commanding officer let my nephew go with instructions not to let anyone know that he had revealed this plot to him. The commanding officer then called for two of the centurions under his command and told them to arrange for 200 soldiers, 70 cavalry, and 200 spearmen to depart for Caesarea between midnight and dawn, placing Paul on a horse for the journey, that they might bring me safely to Felix the Roman governor of Judea. The commanding officer wrote a letter to be presented to Felix saying, 'From Claudius Lysias to your Excellency Governor Felix. Greetings. This man was taken by the Jews, and they would have killed him except for the fact that I came with an army and rescued him, having realized he was a Roman citizen. I brought him before their council, the Sanhedrin, to know the cause for which they were accusing him. What I learned was they were accusing him of matters relating to their religious law, but nothing that justified a penalty of death or imprisonment. Later, when I was informed that the Jews were lying in wait to assassinate the man, I immediately sent him to you and told his accusers to come before you to present what they had against him. Farewell.'

Then the soldiers took me, as they were commanded, and brought me overnight to Antipatris.

"That morning the cavalry took me on to Caesarea while the infantry troops returned to the castle in Jerusalem. When the cavalry arrived in Caesarea with me, they turned over the letter of commanding officer Claudius Lysias and presented me to the governor. After reading the letter, the governor asked what province I was from. When he was informed that I was from Cilicia he said, 'I will hear your case when your accusers come here.' Then he gave commandment that I be held in Herod's judgment hall, since Herod was the local ruler for Judea.

"Five days later, Ananias the high priest came down to Caesarea from Jerusalem together with the other elders of the Sanhedrin. With them was an orator named Tertullus, to speak against me before the governor. When Tertullus was called on he began with words intended to flatter Governor Felix. After such pleasantries, he launched into accusations alleging that I was a pest and was moving Jews throughout the world to sedition as a ringleader of The Way, which is called the sect of the Nazarene. He went on to falsely accuse me of profaning the Temple in Jerusalem. For this alleged offense, which was false, he said the Sanhedrin would have taken me and judged me according to the religious law of the Jews, except for the fact that Lysias, the commanding officer of the Roman garrison came and violently removed me from their hands commanding my accusers to go to the governor. The rejectionist traditional Jews present gave their assent saying it was as Tertullus had presented the argument.

"When Governor Felix beckoned me to speak in my own defense, I noted that the governor had been Rome's authority in the nation for several years and was not a novice in these matters. I went on to say, 'It had only been twelve days since I came to Jerusalem to worship at the Temple. In that time no one found me in the Temple disputing with anyone or stirring up the people whether in the synagogues or around the city. My accusers cannot prove any of the charges they are leveling against me. However, I openly confess that I worship the God of my ancestors in the way they call heresy. It is in this way that I worship the

God of my ancestors, believing everything written in the Law of Moses and in the prophets. My hope in God, which they also ascribe to, is that a resurrection is coming of both the righteous and the unrighteous. This is how I worship with a clear conscience before God and toward men.'

"I went on to say, 'After traveling around the empire of Rome for many years I came back to Jerusalem bringing an offering and donations to my nation. It was then that some Jews from the province of Asia saw me being ceremonially purified in the Temple, without a crowd or tumult. It is they that should have been here to make their case before you governor and should have stated their objections if they had something against me. Since those direct witnesses are not here, let those that are here declare any wrong that I committed when I stood before the Sanhedrin, except for this one thing: I cried out among them regarding the resurrection of the dead. That is the issue before you today.'

"After Governor Felix heard these things, having a more perfect understanding of The Way, he put off a decision with the Sanhedrin, and said to me, 'When Lysias the commanding officer of the garrison comes here, I would like to know the full details of your matter.' He then commanded a centurion to have charge of me, but to allow me liberty with no restrictions on my friends that would come to visit me."

Two Years a Prisoner in Caesarea, But Safe from Assassins

"After some days, Governor Felix came with his wife Drusilla, who was a Jewess. He then sent for me and heard me out concerning faith in Christ. As I reasoned with Felix concerning righteousness, temperance, and the judgment to come, he trembled, and said, 'Go your way for now. When I have a convenient opportunity, I will call you back.'

"Felix also was hoping that I would give him a bribe to gain my freedom. So, Governor Felix sent for me frequently and spent time with me. After two years in that situation, Porcius Festus came in as governor in place of Felix. Felix, wishing to please the Jews, left me bound as he departed.

"Three days after Festus arrived in the province he went up from Caesarea to Jerusalem. There, the high priest, who was the highest ranking among the Jews, gave the new Governor Festus his version of the charges against me and asked Festus to do him the favor of sending me back to Jerusalem to be tried. The high priest did this hoping to revive the conspiracy in which assassins would ambush me to kill me. But Festus preferred that I remain at Caesarea. He intended to go back to Caesarea shortly and invited those members of the Sanhedrin that were willing and able to travel with him and bring their charges against me there."

Paul Appeals to Caesar

"After spending more than ten days in Jerusalem, Festus went back down to Caesarea. The following day he commanded that I be brought before his judgment seat. The Jews which came down from Jerusalem stood by and charged me with many serious offenses but could prove none of them.

"When I answered for myself, I reiterated that I had neither violated the Jewish Law of Moses, profaned the Temple, nor offended Caesar. In fact, I said, 'I have offended in nothing.'

"But Festus, being that he was newly arrived as governor and wanting to build good will with the Jews, turned to me, a Roman citizen, and said, 'Paul, are you willing to go up to Jerusalem and be judged by me there regarding all of these charges?'

"At that point, I said, 'I stand before Caesar's judgment seat, where I should be judged. I have done nothing wrong to the Jews, and you know that full well. If I have broken the law or committed a capital offense worthy of the death penalty, I don't refuse to die. But if none of these things are valid that they are accusing me of doing, then no one can turn me over to them. I am appealing to Caesar.' Governor Festus, wishing to rid himself of this problem he inherited from his predecessor Felix, conferred with the Sanhedrin and addressed me saying, 'So you are appealing to Caesar? Then you will go to Caesar.'

"A few days later, King Herod Agrippa II, who was the grandson of Herod the Great, with his sister and companion Bernice came to Caesarea to make a courtesy call on Festus, the new governor. After Agrippa and Bernice spent many days at Caesarea, Festus informed King Agrippa of my case saying, 'There is a man left in chains by Felix.

When I went up to Jerusalem to acquaint myself with that city and its principals, the chief priests and the other members of the Sanhedrin spoke against the prisoner asking that he be delivered to them for judgment. I told them that it is against Roman justice to turn over a man to face the penalty of death before the one that is being accused can confront his accusers face to face and have the freedom to defend himself against the charges made against him.

"Therefore, when they were come here to Caesarea, I immediately called the case before my judgment seat without delay on the following day and had the man in question brought forth to face his accusers. But when the accusers from Jerusalem took the floor, they didn't bring up any of the things I had expected. Instead, they had questions against him relating to their superstition and of one Jesus, which was dead, but whom Paul affirmed to be alive. Since I was new here and not familiar with these kinds of questions, I asked Paul if he were willing to go up to Jerusalem and be judged there on these charges. But Paul, who is a Roman citizen, appealed for his case to be heard before Nero Claudius Caesar Augustus Germanicus the stepson who succeeded Tiberius Claudius Caesar Augustus Germanicus. Once Paul appealed for his case to be reserved to a hearing by Caesar, I ordered that he be kept here in Caesarea until I had the opportunity to send him to Caesar.'"

Ruins of the Roman Governor's Palace at Caesarea Maratima where Paul Witnessed to two Roman Governors, and to King Herod Agrippa, and was Compelled to Appeal to Caesar.

Paul Witnesses to Herod Agrippa, King of Judea

"Then Agrippa, who was part Jewish and part Idumean, told Festus he would like to hear the man himself. To which Festus agreed to set up a hearing for the next day. King Agrippa and Bernice arrived at the hearing the next day with all their courtiers, military officers, and chief officials of the city in great pomp. I was then brought in at the command of Festus.

"For his part Governor Festus, after acknowledging the presence of King Agrippa and all others present, directed their attention at me saying, 'This is the man that a large group of Jews have besought me both in Jerusalem and here in Caesarea crying out that he doesn't deserve to live a minute longer. But I found that he hadn't done anything deserving of death. Moreover, since he, as a Roman Citizen, appealed to Caesar, that is where I determined to send him. I really don't have anything to write to Caesar, therefore I have brought him out to you, King Agrippa, so that after examining him I might have something

I can write to Caesar, because it just wouldn't be right to send a prisoner to Rome without signifying to Caesar the crimes that have been brought against him.'

"Then King Agrippa, who was the local ruler of the Jews, but collaborated with the Romans, told me I was permitted to speak on my own behalf. I said, 'I am pleased King Agrippa, because I am going to give account today before you of all the things for which the Jews have accused me. I am especially pleased because I know you to be an expert in all of the customs and questions which concern the Jews, therefore, please patiently hear me out.'

"I went on to say, 'All of the Jews know I was brought up among my co-nationals in Jerusalem and lived according to the most conservative and strict sect of our religion as a Pharisee. I stand before you being judged for the hope of the promise God made to our forefathers. It was for this promise that the twelve tribes served God day and night. It is for this that the Jews have accused me King Agrippa. Do you think it is beyond belief that God can raise the dead?' "The truth is I used to think that I should work against the name of Jesus of Nazareth, and I did so in Jerusalem. I shut many of the saints in prison, based on authority I received from the chief priests. When they were put to death, I testified against them and persecuted them in every synagogue, compelling them to blaspheme. I was literally maddened against them and sought them out in foreign cities to persecute them further. It was in pursuit of this that I went to Damascus with a commission and authority from the chief priests.'

"But at midday, my king, I saw on the way to Damascus a light from heaven, brighter than the brightness of the sun, shining all around me and those that journeyed with me. When we had all fallen to the ground from our horses, I heard a voice speaking to me, and saying in Hebrew, 'Saul, Saul, why are you persecuting Me? Isn't it hard for you to kick against the pricks of your conscience?' I said, 'Who are you Lord?'

"He said, 'I am Jesus, the one you are persecuting. Get up on your feet. I have appeared to you for this purpose: to make you a minister and a witness of these things you have seen, and of those things I will show you when I appear to you again. I will deliver you from the people, and from the

Gentiles, to whom I am sending you to open their eyes, turn them from darkness to light, and from the power of Satan unto God, so that they might receive forgiveness of sins, and an inheritance among those that are sanctified by faith in Me.'

"I continued with the king saying, 'After that, King Agrippa, I was not disobedient to the vision from heaven. I presented, first to those of Damascus, and then at Jerusalem and all the borders of Judea, and beyond that to the Gentiles, that they should repent, turn to God, and work the works of repentance. It is for this that the Jews took me in the Temple in Jerusalem and set about to kill me. But I, by the help of God, have continued to this very day, witnessing to men of low degree and those of a high degree saying nothing more than the things which Moses and the prophets said would happen: That Christ should suffer, and that He would be the first one to rise from the dead, and would show His light to the Jewish people and to the Gentiles."

"As I spoke, Governor Festus said with a loud voice, 'You are beside yourself, Paul. Too much learning has made you a mad man.'

"But I retorted, 'I'm not mad, noble Festus, I speak the words of truth and soberness. The king knows about these things, and I speak before him freely. For I am persuaded that none of this has been hidden from him. This was not done in a corner.'

"Then turning to the king, I said, 'King Agrippa, do you believe the prophets? I know that you believe.'

"Then King Agrippa said to me, 'You have almost persuaded me to be a Christian.'

"I responded, 'I would to God, that not only you, but also everyone listening to me today were both almost, and altogether as I am, except these chains.'

"After I had finished speaking, King Agrippa got up together with Governor Festus, Bernice, and the other dignitaries that were with them and went aside out of the judgment seat to confer among themselves. They said, 'This man hasn't done anything to merit death or chains.' Then Agrippa said to Festus, 'This man might have been acquitted and set free, if he had not appealed to Caesar.'"

The Journey to Rome

"When it was determined to have me set sail to Italy, I was delivered, along with some other prisoners, to a centurion named Julius of Augustus' band. Luke and Aristarchus, a Macedonian from Thessalonica, accompanied me as private passengers. The centurion Julius was very courteous toward me and allowed me to go ashore with my friends in Sidon to refresh ourselves. From Sidon we sailed under Cyprus because the winds were against us. Then we came back up over the Sea of Cilicia and Pamphylia to Myra in the province of Lycia. There the centurion found a ship from Alexandria, Egypt, loaded with grain, that was heading to Italy. He had us switch to that ship. It was a bad time of the year to sail on the Great Sea. Again, the winds were against us forcing us to sail under Crete to a place called The Fair Havens. At that point the sailing had become dangerous, but The Fair Havens was not a good port in which to winter.

"I warned them saying, 'Sirs, I see this voyage will suffer hurt and damage, not just of the lading and ship, but also of our lives.' However, the centurion chose to believe the master and owner of the ship, rather than what I had said hoping to make it to a haven on the west of Crete.

"When it appeared that we had obtained a favorable wind, they set sail keeping close to the shoreline of Crete. It wasn't long after setting sail again that we were caught up in a hurricane called Euroclydon. The ship's crew was forced to let the ship drive in the wind.

"Over several days we were tossed around in the sea and lightened the ship including the tackling. We continued in the storm for many days not seeing either the sun or stars and began to lose hope that we would be saved. After holding my peace for a long time, I finally stood up and said, 'Sirs, you should have heeded me and not set out from Crete. You wouldn't have come to this harm and loss. But now I have good news for you. The ship is going to be lost, but no man's life will be forfeit. Last night an angel from God, who I belong to and who I serve, appeared to me and said, 'Don't be afraid, Paul. You have to go before Caesar, and besides that, God has given you the lives of everyone who is sailing with you.' I told all those aboard to cheer up because I believed God that it will be just as it was told to me. However, we will be cast up on an island.

"But, after fourteen nights on the sea in the storm the crew believed we were drawing near land and dropped four anchors out of the stern to keep us from breaking up on yet unseen rocks. When the crew were about to abandon the ship in a lifeboat, feigning to put down anchors from the bow, I told the centurion Julius and his soldiers, 'If these men don't stay in the ship you will die.' The soldiers then quickly cut the ropes of the boat and let it fall into the sea.

"As the day was beginning to dawn, I asked everyone to eat something for their health's sake, because no one had eaten anything for fourteen days. Promising them that not so much as a hair would fall from the head of any of them, I took some bread and gave thanks to God in their presence and began to eat. Then they were all encouraged and every one of the 276 souls on board took something to eat.

"When they had eaten their fill, they threw the wheat cargo into the sea to lighten the ship. When it was day, they didn't know where they were, but seeing a creek and shore they attempted run into the creek with the ship. So, the anchors were taken up, the mainsail was hoisted, the rudders freed, and we made our way toward the shore.

"The ship ran aground with the bow stuck while the stern was being broken up by the waves. The soldiers decided to kill the prisoners to prevent an escape. But Julius the centurion, wishing to save me, kept them from that course of action. He ordered those soldiers that could swim to jump into the sea and swim for the shore first. Then the rest of us, using boards and pieces of the ship could assay to follow them. In that way we all made it safely to land.

"Once we were safely ashore, we learned that we were on the island of Malta. The local people showed us a lot of kindness. They built a fire for us and welcomed everyone because of the rain and the cold. As I gathered a bundle of sticks and placed them on the fire to keep it going, a viper came out from the heat and locked on to my hand with its fangs. The local people, when they saw the venomous snake hanging on my hand said, between themselves, that I must be a murderer, who although managing to avoid drowning at sea was still going to meet a just end by the serpent. But I shook the beast into the fire and felt no harm.

"The local people stared at me for a while expecting me to swell up from the venom or fall dead. When no harm came to me, they came to a different opinion and said I was a god.

"The chief of the island, a man named Publius, received us and lodged us very courteously in some of his nearby properties for three days. The father of Publius was sick with a fever and spitting up blood. When I entered the house he was in, I prayed for him and laying my hands on him, and he was healed. When word of this got out other people on the island that were sick came and were healed. "When the time came for us to depart, the people of the island bestowed many honors on us and gave us provisions necessary to get us on our way.

"After three months on Malta, we departed in another ship from Alexandria, Egypt, which had wintered on the island. The ship's bow spirit were the Roman gods Castor and Pollux. These two were said to be sons of Jupiter, their king of the gods, and were thought to be useful in saving those at sea.

"From Malta we arrived in Sicily, where we remained for three days. From there we sailed along the coast of southern Italy to Rhegium and then to Puteoli near Herculaneum. We found some believers in Puteoli that begged us to stay for a week before we went on by foot toward Rome.

"From there, once other believers heard of us, they came to meet us as far as from Appii Forum and The Three Taverns, both of which were on the Appian Way south of Rome. Seeing this outpouring of love encouraged me greatly. I thanked God for this grace.

Paul's Team Served Him in Rome as He Ministered and Assigned Church Leaders to Other Provinces While Under Guard

"Upon arriving in Rome, Julius the centurion delivered the prisoners to the captain of the guard, but I was allowed to hire a dwelling for myself at my own expense, albeit with a soldier that kept guard. We were able to find a roomy place so that Luke and Aristarchus could also lodge in the same place. In addition, it had ample room to accommodate others who had labored with me and later joined me in Rome, Timothy, Mark, Epaphras, Tychicus, Epaphroditus, and Demas. One Onesimus, who had been a slave of Philemon, also came to be with us and his service to me was most welcome. Unfortunately, Aristarchus was placed in bonds with me. The same condition also befell Epaphras.

"Three days after my arrival in Rome I invited the chiefs of the Jews together. When they were all gathered, I said, 'Men and brothers, even though I committed no wrong against the Jewish people or the traditions of our ancestors, I was still delivered from Jerusalem into the hands of the Romans in Judea. After they examined me, they would have let me go free because there was nothing done by me that was worthy of a death sentence. However, when the Jews of the Sanhedrin spoke against my liberty, I, as a Jew with Roman citizenship, was constrained to appeal to Caesar. That was not because I wanted to accuse my nation of anything. That is why I have called you here to see you and speak to you. It is for the hope of Israel that I am bound with this chain.'

"The Jewish community leaders of Rome said, 'We haven't received letters out of Judaea concerning you and none of the Jewish brothers that came here showed us anything or said anything to harm your reputation. However, we would like to hear your thoughts concerning The Way because we understand that it is spoken against by leaders of synagogues everywhere.'

"So, a day was set to hear me fully. On that day a great many of the Jewish community leaders in Rome came to my hired quarters where I was imprisoned. From morning on to the evening I presented and testified of the kingdom of God, showing how Jesus was spoken of both in the Law of Moses and the prophets. Some believed the things I spoke, and some did not.

"When they couldn't come to agreement among themselves, they prepared to go to their homes. After that, I said this one thing, 'The Holy Ghost spoke a true thing to the prophet Isaiah when He commanded him saying, 'Go to this people, and say, hearing you will hear, and you will not understand, and seeing you will see, and yet you won't perceive. For the heart of this people is hardened, their ears are hard of hearing, and they have shut their eyes; so that they won't see with their eyes, hear with their ears, understand with their heart, and be converted so that I would heal them.'

"Turning to the leaders of the Jewish community in Rome I said, 'Know this one thing, the salvation of God is being sent to the Gentiles, and they will hear it.' When I spoke these final words, the Jews departed and greatly reasoned among themselves.

"For two whole years, I remained in my own hired house in Rome, and received all that came to me, preaching to them the kingdom of God, and teaching those things concerning the Lord Jesus Christ, with all confidence, no man forbidding me. I received all whether slave or free of low degree or high. Members of Caesar's own large household came to me as did officers and soldiers of the Imperial Guard, the Pretorians. The rejectionist traditional Jews and Judaizing Christians that had plagued me everywhere I had gone before were not able to trouble me. With the help of my co-laborers, I wrote letters to the churches at Ephesus and Colossae that were delivered by Tychicus.

"To the church at Ephesus, I said, 'It is my prayer that the God of our Lord Jesus Christ, the Father of glory, would give you the spirit of wisdom and revelation in the knowledge of Him with your understanding being enlightened; that you might know the hope of His calling, and the riches of the glory of His inheritance in the saints, and the exceeding greatness of His power toward we who believe, according to the working of His mighty power, which He wrought in Christ, when He raised Him from the dead, and set Him at his own right hand in heavenly places. A place far above all principality, and power, and might, and dominion, and every name that is named, not only in this world, but also in that which is to come.'

"I reminded them saying, 'Even though you were spiritually dead in your sins, God made you to be alive. You had been dead in sin walking in the way of the world under the sway of the prince of the power of the air, who is the spirit at work in the children of disobedience. You walked among them in the past with your conversations rooted in the lusts of the flesh, fulfilling the desires of the flesh and of the mind, and were by nature the children of wrath. But God, who is rich in mercy, demonstrated His great love for us, even when we were dead in sins, by making us alive together with Christ (by grace we are saved), and raised us up together, and caused us sit together in heavenly places in Christ

Jesus: That in the ages to come He might show the exceeding riches of His grace in His kindness toward us through Christ Jesus. For we are saved by grace through faith, and that not because of anything we have done to merit it. It is the gift of God and not of works, so that no man can boast.'

"I said, 'We are His workmanship, created in Christ Jesus to do good works, which God had pre-ordained that we should walk in good works. In the past, you were non-Jews, aliens concerning the covenants of promise, without hope, and without God. But now, in Christ Jesus, you who used to be far off are brought near by the blood of Christ. He is our peace.'

"Christ Jesus has made both Jew and non-Jew to be one and has broken down the middle wall of partition between us. He abolished, in His flesh, the enmity between the two, even the commandments and ordinances in the Law of Moses, to make in himself, out of two, one new man, and so made peace to the end that He reconciled both to God in one body by the cross, thereby putting an end to the enmity. He preached peace to both those that were far removed and to them that were near the promises. It is through Him that both have access by one Spirit to God the Father. Now because of that you are no longer strangers and foreigners, but fellow citizens with the saints and God's household. You are now built on the foundation of the apostles and prophets, with Jesus Christ Himself being the chief cornerstone. In Him the whole building is tightly held together and is growing into a holy temple in the Lord. In Him you too are built together to be a dwelling place of God through the Spirit."

The Mystery of Christ and of the Gentile Church

"I, Paul, am a prisoner, here in Rome, of Jesus Christ for you non-Jews. Perhaps you have heard of the dispensation of the grace of God which is given me to minister to you. How by revelation God made known to me the mystery of Christ, which in ages past was not known to men as it has now been revealed to His holy apostles and prophets by the Spirit.

"This is the mystery, that the non-Jews should be fellow heirs, and of the same body, and partakers of His promise in Christ by the gospel.

It was because of this revelation I was made a minister, according to the gift of the grace of God given to me by the effectual working of his power. To me, who am less than the least of all saints, is this grace given, that I should preach among the non-Jews the unsearchable riches of Christ. And to make all men see the fellowship of the mystery, which from the beginning of the world has been hid in God, who created all things by Jesus Christ.

"This is to the purpose that you would know the love of Christ, which supersedes knowledge, that you might be filled with all the fullness of God. To Him that is able to do exceedingly abundantly above all that we ask or think, according to the power that works in us, to Him be glory in the church by Christ Jesus throughout all ages, world without end. Amen.

"This Jesus descended to the lower parts of the earth and then ascended on high taking with Him the righteous dead, who had been separated from God. He then ordained that some living in this world should be apostles; some prophets; some evangelists; and some, pastors and teachers, for the perfecting of the saints, for the work of the ministry, and for the edifying of the body of Christ until all of us come in the unity of the faith, and of the knowledge of the Son of God, to a perfect man, to the measure of the stature of the fullness of Christ.

"I delivered instructions to husbands and wives, likening their relationship to that of Christ and the church where Christ is the head of the church and its savior, but so loved the church that He gave himself for it that it would be sanctified and cleansed so that it could be presented to Him as a glorious church without spot or wrinkle or any such thing so that it would be holy and without blemish. I also gave them advice about family relationships. Likewise, I taught them regarding the proper relationships, in Christ, between masters and slaves.

"Finally, I said, 'We aren't wrestling against flesh and blood, but against principalities, against powers, against the rulers of the darkness of this world, and against spiritual wickedness in high places. Therefore, we need to put on the full armor of God so that we can withstand the wiles of the devil and be able to stand in a day when evil rises up.'

"I challenged them to pray always with all prayer and supplication in the Spirit, with an eye to watching, with all perseverance and supplication, for all of the saints. Further, to pray for me that I would open my mouth boldly, to make known the mystery of the gospel, for which I am an ambassador in chains, that, though a prisoner, I may speak boldly, as I ought to speak.

"In my letter to the church at Colossae, which was also for the church at Laodicea, I wrote about the Godhead. I also sent a letter to the church at Laodicea with instructions for the two churches the share the letters with each other. I said, 'God delivered us from the power of darkness and translated us into the kingdom of His dear Son Jesus Christ.'

"Our redemption is through His blood, even the forgiveness of sins. Our Lord Jesus, who walked among us, is the image of the invisible God, the firstborn of every creature. Everything created in heaven, and on earth, visible and invisible, whether thrones, or dominions, or principalities, or powers; all things were created by Him, and for Him.

"Jesus Christ was before all things, and by Him all things consist. He is the head of the body, the church: who is the beginning, and the firstborn from the dead; that in all things He might have the preeminence. It pleased the Father that in Jesus Christ the Son should all fullness should dwell. Having made peace through the blood of His cross, by Him God reconciled all things unto Himself, whether they be things in earth, or things in heaven. And you, who were once alienated and enemies in your mind by wicked works, yet now he has reconciled you. He did this in His body of flesh, through death, to present you holy and unblameable and unreproveable in His sight.

"To the churches at Colossae and Laodicea, I said, 'I had been made a minister, according to the dispensation of God that He gave me for them, to fulfill the word of God. Yes, the mystery that had been hid from ages past and from generations, but now is made known to His saints. To whom God would make known the riches of the glory of this mystery among the non-Jews, which is Christ in you, the hope of glory. This is what we preach, warning every man, and teaching every man in all wisdom; that we may present every man perfect in Christ Jesus.

"In a rebuke to the Christian Judaizers, I said, 'You of the churches at Colossae and Laodicea are indeed circumcised, but with a circumcision made without hands, in putting off the body of the sins of the flesh by the circumcision of Christ. You were buried with Him in baptism and risen with Him through the faith of the operation of God, who has raised Him from the dead. And you, who had been dead in your sins and the uncircumcision of your flesh, He made alive together with Him, having forgiven you all trespasses by blotting out the handwriting of ordinances that was against us, which was contrary to us, and took them out of the way, nailing them to His cross. Having spoiled principalities and powers, He made an open show of them, triumphing over them in it.'

"'Since you are thus risen with Christ, seek those things which are above, where Christ sits on the right hand of God. Set your affections on things above, not on things on the earth. For their old life is dead, and their new life is hidden with Christ in God. When Christ, who is our life, appears, then we will also appear with Him in glory.'

"Therefore, I charged them to put to death in their fleshly bodies on earth fornication, uncleanness, inordinate affection, evil strong sexual lust, and covetousness, which is idolatry. It is because of these things that the wrath of God comes on the children of disobedience. I said, 'But now you should also put off anger, wrath, malice, blasphemy, and filthy communication out of your mouth. Don't lie to one another, seeing that you have put off the old man along with his deeds and have put on the new man, which is renewed in knowledge after the image of Him that created the new man; where there is neither non-Jew nor Jew, circumcision nor uncircumcision, Barbarian, Scythian, slave nor free, but Christ is all, and in all.'

"I concluded by addressing relationships within families, and relationships between slaves and masters. I said, 'You should remember to pray, and especially for us, that God would open a door of utterance, for us to speak the mystery of Christ, for which reason I was also in chains in Rome. I closed by commending to them my many helpers and co-laborers, including those that were from Colossae.

"To Philemon, I wrote a letter delivered by Onesimus and Tychicus. In that letter I asked Philemon to receive Onesimus, the former runaway slave, not as a slave again, but as a brother for the sake of love, and to charge any debt to my account. Onesimus ministered to me during my imprisonment in Rome, and I would have had him continue in such service, but it had to come willingly from Philemon, who had been wronged by Onesimus.

"The church in Philippi sent a gift by the hands of Epaphroditus that enabled us to continue working from the hired house in Rome. I wrote the church in Philippi a letter, together with Timothy, in part to thank them for their gift. When Epaphroditus, who had been sick near death, recovered, he carried my letter back to the church at Philippi. The churches there sent representatives to inform me of the state of affairs in the churches I had planted. In my letter I saluted the bishops and deacons that we had appointed and sought to have them understand that the things which had happened to me, including my imprisonment in Rome, have fallen out to the furtherance of the gospel.

"I said, 'My chains for the cause of Christ are well known in all of Caesar's palace, and in all other places. Also, many of the brethren in the Lord have become confident because of my chains and have become bolder to speak the word without fear. I know that this situation will turn out to my deliverance through your prayer, and the supply of the Spirit of Jesus Christ, according to my earnest expectation and my hope, that shall not be ashamed in anything, but that with all boldness, as always, so now also Christ shall be magnified in my body, whether it be by my living, or by my death.'

"'For me to continue living honors Christ, and to die would be my gain. But if I live in the flesh, this is the fruit of my labor. Yet I don't know which to choose. For I am in a strait between two options, having a desire to depart, and to be with Christ, which is far better for me. Nevertheless, to stay here in the flesh is more helpful to you. I am confident that I shall abide and continue with you all for your furtherance and joy of faith. That your rejoicing may be more abundant in Jesus Christ for me by my coming to you again.'

"'Don't be terrified by your adversaries, which is to them an evident token of their damnation, but to you of salvation, and that of God.

For to you it is given on the behalf of Christ, not only to believe on him, but also to suffer for his sake.

"I said, 'Let the mind be in you, which was also in Christ Jesus, who, being in the form of God, did not think it robbery to be equal with God, but made Himself of no reputation, and took upon Him the form of a servant, and was made in the likeness of men. Having been found in fashion as a man, He humbled Himself, and became obedient unto death, even the death of the cross. Because of that God also has highly exalted Him and given Him a name that is above every name. That at the name of Jesus every knee should bow, of things in heaven, and things on earth, and things under the earth, that every tongue should confess that Jesus Christ is Lord, to the glory of God the Father. Wherefore, my beloved, work out your own salvation with fear and trembling. For it is God which works in you both to will and to do of his good pleasure.'"

Paul Extols Timothy

"Commending Timothy, I said, 'I hoped in the Lord Jesus to send Timothy shortly to you, that I also may be of good comfort, when I learn of your state. For I don't have another likeminded man who will naturally care for your state. For all seek their own, not the things which are Jesus Christ's.'

"But you know the proof of Timothy, that, as a son with his father, he has served with me in the gospel. Therefore, I hope to send Timothy to you as soon as I see how it will go with me. But I am still trusting in the Lord that I also myself shall come to you shortly.

"Yet I supposed it necessary to send to you, without delay, Epaphroditus, my brother, and companion in labor, and fellow soldier, but your messenger, and he that ministered to my wants. He was sick and nearly died, but God had mercy on him, and not on him only, but on me also, lest I should have sorrow upon sorrow. Receive him therefore in the Lord with all gladness, and hold him in reputation, because for the work of Christ he was nigh unto death, not regarding his life, to supply your lack of service toward me.

"Evaluating myself, I said, 'The things I once gloried in as a Pharisee I counted as loss in exchange for the excellency of the knowledge of

Christ Jesus my Lord, for whom I have suffered the loss of all things, and consider those things equivalent to dung, that I may win Christ, and be found in him, not having my own righteousness, which is based on the law, but that which is through the faith of Christ, the righteousness which is of God by faith. That I might know Him, and the power of His resurrection, and the fellowship of His sufferings, being made conformable unto His death, if by any means I might attain unto the resurrection of the dead. I speak not as though I have already attained my goals, or either were already perfect, but I follow after, if that I may apprehend that for which also I am apprehended of Christ Jesus.'

"'Brothers,' I said, 'I don't consider myself to have already apprehended my goal, but this one thing I do, forgetting those things which are behind, and reaching forth unto those things which are before, I press toward the mark for the prize of the high calling of God in Christ Jesus. Let us therefore, as many as would be perfect, be thus minded.

"'Finally,' I said, 'the church at Philippi should rejoice in the Lord always.' And again, I said, 'Rejoice. Let your moderation be known to all men. The Lord's return is at hand.

"'In conclusion, I said, 'You should be anxious for nothing, but in everything by prayer and supplication with thanksgiving let your requests be made known unto God. And the peace of God, which passes all understanding, will keep your hearts and minds through Christ Jesus. Whatever things are true, whatever things are honest, whatever things are just, whatever things are pure, whatever things are lovely, whatever things are of good report; if there be any virtue in them, and if there be any praise, think on these things. Those things, which you have both learned, and received, and heard, and seen in me, do them and the God of peace shall be with you.'"

Acquitted and Set Free to Continue His Ministry from Country to Country

"Later, I sent Timothy to Philippi, and he went on to Ephesus from there. When my accusers from Jerusalem did not come to press their case against me, I was eventually acquitted and set free. In that time, I went to Spain to preach there and go on to other places.

"Although I thought I would witness before Caesar, it did not happen during my imprisonment, at least not at that time. I used my freedom to return to Macedonia to see to the needs of the churches there and to personally thank the church at Philippi for its financial support.

"While in Macedonia I wrote a letter to Timothy. I called Timothy my son in the Spirit. I wrote that I thanked Christ Jesus our Lord, for putting me into the ministry. Previously, I was a blasphemer, and a persecutor, and injurious, but I obtained mercy, because I did it ignorantly in unbelief. Christ Jesus came into the world to save sinners, of whom I am chief. I received mercy so that Jesus Christ might, in me, show His longsuffering, as an example for them that would afterwards believe on Him to receive everlasting life.

"I charged my son Timothy, according to the prophecies which he had received so that by them he might war a good warfare. I urged him, first of all, that supplications, prayers, intercessions, and giving of thanks, be made for all men, for kings, and for all that are in authority, that we may lead a quiet and peaceable life in all godliness and honesty. Because God our Savior would have all men to be saved, and to come to the knowledge of the truth. For there is one God, and one mediator between God and men, the man Christ Jesus, Who gave himself a ransom for all.

"It was for this I was ordained a preacher, and an apostle (I speak the truth in Christ, and I am not lying), and a teacher of the Gentiles in faith and truthfulness. I would, therefore, that men pray everywhere, lifting up holy hands, without wrath and doubting.

"Instructions were given to Timothy on appointing bishops and elders in the churches. I said, 'It is a good thing for a man to desire the office of a bishop, but a bishop then must be blameless, the husband of one wife, vigilant, sober, of good behavior, given to hospitality, apt to teach, not given to wine, not quick to throw a punch, not greedy for self-enrichment, but patient, not a brawler, not covetous; one that rules his own house well, having his children in subjection with all gravity.

For if a man doesn't know how to rule his own house, how can he take care of the church of God? He must not be a novice, lest being lifted up with pride he should fall into the condemnation of the devil. Moreover, he must have a good report of them which are outside the church, lest in this situation too he should fall into reproach and the snare of the devil.

"'Likewise, deacons must be grave, not speaking out of both sides of their mouths, not given to too much wine, not greedy in search of self-enrichment, holding the mystery of the faith in a pure conscience. And let these also first be tested during a probationary period; then let them use the office of a deacon, having been found blameless. Even so must their wives be grave, not slanderers, sober, faithful in all things. Let the deacons be the husbands of one wife, ruling their children and their own houses well. For they that have used the office of a deacon well purchase to themselves a good degree, and great boldness in the faith which is in Christ Jesus.'

"Regarding my travels, I said, 'I hoped to come to Ephesus to see my son in the Spirit soon, but if my coming should be delayed, I wanted you to know how to behave yourself in the house of God, which is the church of the living God, the pillar and ground of the truth. Without controversy, great is the mystery of godliness: God was manifest in the flesh, justified in the Spirit, seen of angels, preached to the Gentiles, believed on in the world, and received up into glory.'"

Warning of the Coming Apostasy and the Need to Establish Bishops, Elders, and Deacons

"The Spirit had spoken expressly, 'That in the last days some shall depart from the faith, giving heed to seducing spirits, and doctrines of devils. They will hypocritically speak lies because their consciences are as seared with a hot iron. They will forbid marriage, and command all to abstain from eating meat, which God has created to be received with thanksgiving by them that believe and know the truth. Every creature of God is good, and nothing is to be refused, if it is received with thanksgiving, for it is sanctified by the word of God and prayer.

"As for additional advice to Timothy, I said, 'Give sound teaching to those in the church,' and I provided some fatherly advice on how to keep himself. I said, 'Let no man despise your youth, but be an example of the believers, in word, in conversation, in love, in spirit, in faith, and in purity.'

"Until I get back to Ephesus, I urged him to give attention to reading the scriptures, to exhortation, and to doctrine, not neglecting the gift of the Spirit in him that was given him by prophecy, and the laying on of the hands of the presbytery. 'Meditate on these things,' I said. 'Give yourself wholly to them that your profiting in this may be readily seen by all.'

"Further, I gave Timothy advice on how to deal with aged men and widows. Likewise, I gave instruction on how to administer elders who are helping to oversee the church.

"On keeping oneself, I wrote on the necessity for all to live godly lives and to be content, for the love of money is the root of all evil: which when some coveted after money, they departed from the faith, and brought many regrets upon themselves. I said, 'But you, man of God, flee these things, and follow after righteousness, godliness, faith, love, patience, and meekness. Fight the good fight of faith, laying hold on eternal life, to which you are also called, and have professed a good profession before many witnesses. I charge you in the sight of God, who gives life to all things, and before Christ Jesus, who before Pontius Pilate gave witness of a good confession, that you keep my charge to you without spot, unrebukable, until the appearing of our Lord Jesus Christ, which in His times He shall reveal Himself as the blessed and only Potentate, the King of kings, and Lord of lords, who alone is immortal, dwelling in the light that no man can come near, whom no man has seen, nor can see, to Whom be honor and power everlasting.

"I commanded Timothy to charge them that are rich in this world, that they be not high-minded, nor trust in uncertain riches, but in the living God, who gives us richly all things to enjoy, that they do good, and that they be rich in good works, ready to distribute, willing to communicate, thus laying up in store for themselves a good foundation against the time to come, that they may lay hold on eternal life.

"From Macedonia, I crossed over to the province of Asia and returned to Ephesus. I had sent word to Timothy to remain in Ephesus to combat false doctrines while I went through Macedonia. It was good to reunite with my son in the Spirit in Ephesus.

"After a season in Ephesus and the province of Asia, I went to Crete with Titus and Luke, and left Titus in Crete to carry on there. I eventually sent another co-laborer to Crete to care for the church, along with a letter I wrote to Titus, so that Titus could meet me in Nicopolis.

"My letter to Titus recognized him as my own son after the common faith. I reminded Titus that I left him in Crete to put things in order that were lacking in the church and to ordain elders in every city on the island as I had given him authority to do. I then laid out for him the qualities each elder needed to satisfy. "I said, 'A bishop must blameless, the husband of one wife, with faithful children not accused of riotous or unruly living. As God's steward, a bishop needs a temperament that is not self-willed, not quick to be angry, not given to too much wine, not a brawler, and not one to seek self-enrichment. Such a man must love showing hospitality, be a lover of good men, sober, just, holy, and temperate. A bishop, moreover, must hold fast to the faithful word that he has been taught by us that he may be able, by sound doctrine, to exhort and convince disagreeable persons that attempt to contradict his message.' "I said this to Titus because the Cretans are known to have many among them that are unruly, vain talkers, and deceivers. This is especially true of the rejectionist traditional Jews among them. The mouths of such people must be stopped, because they would subvert whole households, teaching things which they shouldn't in order to get money for themselves through their deceit and opposition to the truth.

"I also gave Titus instruction to speak giving sound doctrine. That the old men be sober, grave, temperate, sound in their faith, in love, and in patience. Likewise, the older women should be admonished to behave as becomes holiness, not falsely accusing others, not given to too much wine, and be teachers of good things so they can likewise teach the young women to be sober, to love their husbands, to love their children, be discreet, chaste, keep at home, be good, and obedient to their own husbands, so that the word of God is not harmed and blasphemed by their actions. The young should likewise be exhorted to be sober minded.

"Regarding the relationship between slaves and masters, I said, 'Exhort slaves to be obedient to their own masters, and to please them well in all things; not backtalking; not stealing but showing themselves to be faithful, that they may adorn the doctrine of God our Savior in all things.

"For the grace of God that brings salvation has appeared to all men, teaching us that, denying ungodliness and worldly lusts, we should live soberly, righteously, and godly, in this present world, looking for that blessed hope, and the glorious appearing of the great God and our Savior, Jesus Christ, who gave Himself for us, that he might redeem us from all iniquity, and purify to Himself a peculiar people, who are zealous to perform good works.

"These things speak, and exhort, and rebuke with all authority. Don't let anyone despise you. In all things show yourself to be an example of good works, in doctrine showing yourself to be uncorruptible, grave, and sincere. Use sound speech, authoritatively, that cannot be condemned, so that anyone that is opposing you may be ashamed, because he would be unable to bring any disparaging charge against you.

"Put everyone in a frame of mind to be subject to principalities and powers, to obey magistrates, and be ready to every good work. To speak evil of no one, not to be brawlers, but gentle, showing meekness to all men. For we ourselves used to be foolish, disobedient, deceived, serving various lusts and pleasures, living in malice and envy, hateful, and hating one another.

"But after the kindness and love of God our Savior toward man appeared, not by works of righteousness which we have done, but according to His mercy He saved us, by the washing of regeneration, and renewing of the Holy Ghost which He abundantly spread over us through Jesus Christ our Savior, so that being justified by His grace, we should be made heirs according to the hope of eternal life.

"In the meantime, I journeyed to Spain to preach Jesus Christ there. Coming back from Spain, I went to Corinth in the company of Luke and

Erastus. I left Erastus in Corinth to provide leadership for that church. From thence I went to Troas with Luke and then to Ephesus to spend time with Timothy and strengthen the church there with sound doctrine."

Arrested Again and Taken Back to Rome

"While in the province of Asia, the rejectionist traditional Jewish leaders again stirred up the authorities against me alleging I was leading people in opposition to Rome's authority, not as if they really cared for Rome. They were no different than the high priests in Jerusalem who called for the crucifixion of Jesus saying to Pilate, the Roman procurator, 'We have no king other than Caesar.'

"Because of them I was arrested and taken by ship to Rome from Miletus. Trophimus was sick and had to be left behind in Miletus. Luke continued with me to Rome. Later, Onesiphorus came to Rome to comfort me also. The work was not limited to me or to where I was free to go. Crescens went to Galatia and Titus went on to Dalmatia. However, Demas left me and the work of the gospel for the things of this world and went to Thessalonica on his own account. "As before, I was able to hire a house for my imprisonment at Rome awaiting a hearing before Nero, the current Caesar. I wrote a second letter to Timothy. I reminded Timothy that I was an apostle of Jesus Christ by God's will and by the life that is in Christ Jesus. I addressed Timothy as my dearly beloved son; speaking over him grace, mercy, and peace, from God the Father and Christ Jesus our Lord. I let him know that I was praying for him night and day.

"To Timothy, I said, 'I greatly desired to see you because I am aware of your tears for me as a prisoner of Rome once again, so that I might be filled with joy upon seeing you again.' I called to remembrance the unfeigned faith in him, which was first in his grandmother Lois, and his mother Eunice, and I was persuaded was also in him. Once again, I reminded Timothy to boldly stir up the gift of God that was in him from the laying on of hands. For God has not given us the spirit of fear, but of power, and of love, and of a sound mind.

"I urged Timothy to neither be ashamed to witness of our Lord, nor of me because I am imprisoned for Him, but be a partaker of the afflictions of the gospel according to the power of God, who has saved us, and called us with a holy calling, not according to our works, but according to His own purpose and grace, which was given us in Christ Jesus before the world began, but is now made manifest by the appearing of our Savior Jesus Christ in human flesh, who abolished death, and has brought life and immortality to light through the gospel. It is for this that I was appointed a preacher, and an apostle, and a teacher of the Gentiles. It is for this calling that I also suffer these things. Nevertheless, I am not ashamed, for I know whom I have believed and am persuaded that He is able to keep that which I have committed unto Him against that appointed day.

"Timothy already knew of all those in the province of Asia that had turned away from me, including Phygellus and Hermogenes. I said, 'But I pray the Lord's mercy on the household of Onesiphorus because he refreshed me often and was not ashamed of my chains. When he was in Rome, he sought me out very diligently, and found me. May the Lord grant him mercy on the day of judgment. You know well how he ministered to me when I was in Ephesus.

"So, my son, I said, 'Be strong in the grace that is in Christ Jesus. And the things that you have heard of me from many witnesses, commit the same to faithful men, who will also be able to teach them to others. Therefore, endure hardness, as a good soldier of Jesus Christ.

"'Consider what I say, and may the Lord give you understanding in all things. Remember Jesus Christ of the seed of David was raised from the dead according to my gospel. It is because of my gospel that I suffer troubles, as though I were an evil doer, even put in chains, but the word of God is not bound. Therefore, I endure all things for the elect's sakes, that they may also obtain the salvation which is in Christ Jesus with eternal glory.

"'This is a faithful saying: If we are dead with Him, we shall also live with Him. If we suffer, we shall also reign with Him. If we deny Him, He also will deny us. If we don't believe, He still remains faithful;

He cannot deny Himself. "I told Timothy, 'Put the people in remembrance of these things. Study to show yourself approved unto God, a workman that doesn't need to be ashamed, rightly dividing the word of truth. Although some have erred and perverted the truth, weakening the faith of some, the foundation of God stands sure, having this seal, the Lord knows them that are His. And, let everyone that names the name of Christ depart from iniquity. But in a great house there are not only vessels of gold and of silver, but also of wood and of earth; some to honor, and some to dishonor.

"'If a man will therefore purge himself from these, he shall be a vessel unto honor, sanctified, and meet for the master's use, and prepared for every good work. Flee also youthful lusts, but rather follow righteousness, faith, love, peace, with them that call on the Lord out of a pure heart. The servant of the Lord must not strive, but be gentle to all men, apt to teach, and patient.'

"Concerning what to expect after my death, I said to Timothy, 'In the last days, perilous times will come. Men will be lovers of their own selves, covetous, boasters, proud, blasphemers, disobedient to parents, unthankful, unholy, without natural affection, trucebreakers, false accusers, incontinent, fierce, despisers of those that are good, traitors, heady, high-minded, and lovers of pleasures more than lovers of God. Such men will have a form of godliness but deny the power thereof. Turn away from such people. For these sort of persons are they which creep into houses, and lead captive silly women laden with sins, led away with various lusts, ever learning, but never able to come to the knowledge of the truth. "'As Jannes and Jambres withstood Moses, so these also resist the truth: men of corrupt minds, reprobate concerning the faith. But you have fully known my doctrine, my manner of life, purpose, faith, longsuffering, love, and patience. You know the persecutions and afflictions, which came upon me at Antioch, at Iconium, and at Lystra. You know the persecutions I endured, but out of them all the Lord delivered me. Yes, and all that will live godly in Christ Jesus will suffer persecution.

"'Although evil men and seducers will wax worse and worse, deceiving, and being deceived, see that you continue in the things that you have learned and have been assured of, knowing of whom you learned them. From your childhood you have known the Holy Scriptures, which are able to make you wise unto salvation through faith which is in Christ Jesus. All scripture is given by inspiration of God, and is profitable for doctrine, for reproof, for correction, and for instruction in righteousness: that the man of God may be perfect and thoroughly furnished unto all good works.'"

Ready to Die for Christ

"Finally, I charged Timothy, therefore before God, and the Lord Jesus Christ, who shall judge the quick and the dead at his appearing and his kingdom, saying, 'Preach the word; be instant in season, out of season; reprove, rebuke, exhort with all longsuffering and doctrine. For the time will come when they will not endure sound doctrine, but after their own lusts shall they heap to themselves teachers, having itching ears. And they shall turn away their ears from the truth and shall be turned unto fables. But see that you watch in all things, endure afflictions, do the work of an evangelist, and make full proof of your ministry. For I am now ready to be offered, and the time of my departure is at hand.'

"I said, 'I have fought a good fight. I have finished my course, I have kept the faith, henceforth there is laid up for me a crown of righteousness, which the Lord, the righteous judge, shall give me at that day, and not to me only, but unto all them also that love His appearing.'

"I concluded by asking Timothy to diligently make haste to come to me quickly because Demas had forsaken me, having loved this present world, and left to go to Thessalonica; Crescens went to Galatia, and Titus went to Dalmatia. Only Luke remained with me. I asked Timothy to take Mark, and bring him with him to Rome, for he is profitable to me for the ministry. I let Timothy know I had sent Tychicus to Ephesus to watch over that church while he comes to me in Rome.

"I also asked him to bring my books and parchments and to bring the heavy cloak that I left in Troas."

CHAPTER 11

From Monuments to Men to the Church Built on the Foundation of Jesus Christ

Timothy and Mark arrived in Rome with Paul's books and parchments and his much-needed heavy cloak. As they sat together with Luke and other believers that had ministered with them, Paul spoke.

Paul announced, "My time will soon end. I know from visitations from the Lord Jesus that Rome is where I would testify of Jesus Christ before Caesar and give my life as my final service and sacrifice."

Turning to Timothy and Mark, Paul said, 'You know that Peter is also imprisoned here in Rome. It may be that we will both give up our lives here. You, Timothy and Mark, and the other younger leaders like Titus and Clement, including women like Priscilla, Phoebe, Lydia, and Junia represent the next generation. The apostle James, John's brother, was beheaded in Jerusalem by Herod. Both I, Peter, and the other apostles are all marked for death. But you must carry on and continue to build on the foundation of Jesus Christ. If necessary, raise up others to carry on after you should the Lord delay His return for His saints."

"Mark spoke up saying, 'Since arriving in Rome, I have been to see Peter who is now at the Mamertine Prison at the Imperial Forum awaiting his own hearing before Nero. Peter has been like a father to me and mentored me just as you have done so with Timothy and others. He too is ready to be faithful unto death."

"'Did you see the gigantic sixty-cubit high statue of Nero near his massive palace, the Domus Aurea, built on land cleared after the great fire?'

Paul said. 'Nero fancies himself to be the sun god in human flesh. Just as their sun god Sol is represented in a chariot, Nero dresses as the sun god and drives his chariot around his private circuit. That bronze statue, with its crown representing rays of light, as the sun god is represented, will not remain. The Domus Aurea will not remain, and Nero will not remain, but our Lord Jesus Christ, whom the Holy Spirit raised from the dead with resurrection power, is alive and will remain forever. And we, if we are found faithful, whether alive or dead, will join Him in the place He has prepared for us.

"'Those dead Caesars whom the Roman Senate calls divine and sons of god, will one day stand to be judged by the saints to give account of their deeds.'

"Mark replied, 'That statue, which is larger than any statue but the Colossus of Rhodes, is no different than the statue of a comparable size set up by Nebuchadnezzar of the Chaldeans near Babylon. Just as Daniel's Hebrew companions refused to put that king above our God, believers in the Lord Jesus Christ will not honor that abomination, even at the cost of their lives. Already, Nero is stirring the people of Rome up against Christ followers and traditional Jews to deflect attention from himself since some have blamed him for the great fire. There is also the beginning of a new uprising in Judea against the Roman occupiers of our land. No doubt, this will add to the climate of harshness against Judea, traditional Jews, and both Jewish and non-Jewish Christians that call Jesus Christ Lord.'

Marcus interrupted, 'Sir, I have heard that Caesar is soon to have you and the prisoner you call Peter appear before him at his judgment seat in the Imperial Forum. I now profess that I believe Jesus Christ, the resurrected savior, is my God and savior who takes away my sins. This I boldly say before you all. I am ready to give my life, if required, to free you and assist your escape from Rome. I am a soldier, and I will gladly war for you Paul.

Paul responded, 'Brother Marcus, welcome to the family! We will baptize you this day with such water as we have available here. However, Jesus Himself has appeared to me several times to make me know that

I will surely give my life here at Rome after witnessing to Caesar. I will not frustrate the wisdom and plan of God by attempting to save myself. Before you came here Marcus, a group of the Pretorians, who are believers, also came to me and offered, as men of war, to free me. I thanked them but declined their offer as I decline yours.'

"Jesus permitted neither Peter's sword nor twelve legions of powerful angels to save Him from His own trial unto death on a cross, the Just One for the unjust. I am not better than my Lord and Master that I should escape death at the hands of unbelievers. Besides, the Holy Spirit has shown me that persecutions, including death for many, are coming for believers soon and for years to come. I dare not weaken their resolve in the hour of their coming trial by fleeing the sentence of death soon to be imposed on me."

A few days later, Paul was transferred to the Mamertine prison and out of the care of Marcus. Marcus allowed Luke, Timothy, and Mark to walk with them to the Mamertine Prison. After many tears and final embraces, Paul was turned over to another soldier and placed in confinement with Peter. There the two Christian warriors and apostles of Jesus Christ shared stories of the great things that had been done in their ministries by the power of the Holy Spirit and how they had been directed by the Holy Spirit to come to Rome to be witnesses of the Lord Jesus Christ before Caesar, the cruel emperor of much of the world.

Peter and Paul Stiffen Each Other's Resolve

"Peter," said Paul, "I have suffered much over the years from traditional Jews that reject the gospel of Jesus Christ. It has also been a battle to keep the faith of the Gentile believers pure notwithstanding the confusion sown by Christian Judaizers who insisted that the grace made possible by the death and resurrection of Jesus Christ was not enough, but that Gentile believers also needed to keep the Law of Moses and the traditions of Jewish people beyond what James and the Council at Jerusalem agreed and sent forth by apostolic letters." Peter answered, "We have new wine that the old wineskins can't contain. I too have had to reprove the misguided Christian Judaizers. We both have had to contend against the heresies of this age that have come to sow confusion in the church.

In addition, the ruler of darkness in this world has already killed James, by Herod's sword, and our deacon Stephen by stoning, as you well know. Now the Holy Spirit has revealed to me that persecutions and much death are at hand for times to be determined."

A Lower Interior Cell of the Mamertine Prison, believed to be the Final Holding Place for Paul and Peter. In the Modern Memorial to the two Apostles, Note the Upside Down Cross.

Peter continued, "I know my time is upon me. One of my Roman soldier prison guards sought to free me, and I went along with his plan. I regret that he and his family were later put to death for this effort. As I made my way south on the Appian Way beyond the walls of Rome, I had an open vision of Jesus walking past me headed the other way. When I denied Him with curses His eyes locked with mine and I was overcome with grief at my betrayal of Him. This time, He didn't even pause to look at me, but walked past me set on going to Rome. I said, 'Lord, where are You going?' In the vision, He responded, without even turning His head back toward me, but answered while still fixed on going to Rome, 'I am going to Rome to be crucified again.' Then the vision vanished. I felt ashamed at that point, turned around and headed back to Rome."

Inscription on a Church in the Appian Way Thought to be where Peter had a Vision of Jesus heading toward Rome.

"As our Lord Jesus said when we walked with Him, 'The one who would follow Me must pick up his own cross and follow Me.' I am back here to bear my own cross. Again, as Jesus once said, 'A grain of wheat will not bring forth unless it falls to the ground and dies.' Paul, it appears that you and I are soon to be sown in death to bring forth a harvest of many more believers, each of whom will be faithful to the point of death, if needs be. This journey does not end with our demise. If so, then Jesus suffered and died for nothing. No, His kingdom will grow and endure forever. We are just stones built on the foundation that Jesus is the Christ, the Son of the Living God. For my part, I am unworthy to be crucified in the same manner as was my Master."

Paul ended saying, "Let's sing a hymn that Silas and I sang in the prison at Philippi in Macedonia after being beaten for being witnesses of the good news and exposing gods made by the hands of men as no gods at all."

Their husky voices echoed through the chamber of that prison. Luke, Timothy, and Mark, standing vigil in the night not far off, heard the hymn being sung in Hebrew, and joined in, tears streaming down their cheeks.

CHAPTER 12

From a Persecutor to an Apostle Boldly Witnessing to Caesar

This was the moment Paul had been waiting for since he encountered the risen Jesus on the road to Damascus. He was in chains as his guard walked him out of the Mamertine Prison to stand by as Nero Caesar made his way on a chariot coming down from his massive Domus Aurea palace, meaning the Golden House. Paul could see Nero's entourage making its way to the judgment seat. Off to the side was the colossal bronze statue of Nero looming large in the distance. Finally, Nero arrived and took his seat with a blare of trumpets. Nero signaled for the prisoner to be brought forth.

As Paul made his way before the judgment seat escorted by a soldier that was guarding him, his rattling chains were the only noise as all around became silent. "Paul," said Nero, "you are a Roman citizen accused by many of subverting Rome and my rule saying there is another king, one Christ, put to death by our procurator in Judea, but whom you say still lives. Do you not recognize my rule in this realm that encircles the Great Sea and extends to lands and peoples beyond? And are you not willing to present offerings to the gods of Rome, including my predecessors as Caesar whom the Senate of Rome has declared to be divine?"

Paul Witnesses to Nero Caesar

Paul responded, "Your excellency, I have done no wrong to you or to Rome. My Lord and Savior Jesus of Nazareth, called the Christ, said, 'Give

Caesar that which belongs to him, and to God those things that belong to Him.' Worship belongs to God alone and I worship Him according to His revelation to my ancestors. In these days He has revealed Himself further by sending His son, Jesus of Nazareth, born of a virgin, having left behind His glory and honor in heaven, to live a blameless life by the power of the Holy Spirit, doing good and taking on the sins of the world on a cross where He died and, after three days, rose and showed Himself with many infallible proofs to many witnesses before being received up into heaven.

"At first, I persecuted those that worshiped Jesus as the Christ promised by God. Then, with letters of authority in hand from the high priests and the elders of the Sanhedrin in Jerusalem, I set out to Damascus, Syria to find and bring back bound to Jerusalem those that worshipped according to The Way, recognizing Jesus as the Christ. But, before I arrived at the city, this Jesus appeared to me in a great light, knocking me and my companions to the ground from our horses, asking why I was persecuting Him. I acknowledged Him as my Lord and asked Him what I needed to do. He told me to go on to Damascus where more would be revealed to me. I went to Damascus still blind from the great light. After three days fasting from food and water, a man, who had himself heard from God, came to me, prayed for me, and caused scales to fall from my eyes so that I could see again, and baptized me in the name of Jesus.

"Since then I have traveled, starting in Damascus, to Roman provinces and islands around the Great Sea as far as Spain preaching the good news of forgiveness of sins and the promise of resurrected eternal life in heaven to those that, by faith, believe in Jesus Christ and are thus justified and made righteous by His sacrifice to redeem us from the darkness and power of this world to be fit to live with Him forever in heaven. Of these things I gladly witness, and it is my prayer that all that hear me this day would believe and receive this precious gift."

Nero responded, "Paul, you have wearied me with these tales. Look around you at mighty Rome and the empire that I rule. Does your heaven have palaces as grand as my Domus Aurea on the hill yonder?

You stand before me in chains. Your life is in my hands, and you dare presume that your words could persuade me or my subjects to become devotees of the one called Christ? Our gods are Jupiter, the king of the gods, Mars the god of war who has helped us conquer the world, and many more including Diana, the goddess worshipped throughout the world and of whom it is reported from the province of Asia, that you have turned many from her upsetting the order of that great city Ephesus and have done likewise in Galatia, Macedonia, Achaia, Syria, and many other provinces. I myself am as a god to the people. Look at my statue gleaming in the sun behind you. All of this glory is mine. You have nothing to offer.

"Now you will cease to turn our provinces, traditions, and worship upside down with your claims of this Christ. But, to show you my power and goodness, I will set you free, if you would now renounce Christ, bow before me as your lord and Divi Filius—son of god—and toward my statue, burning incense at my altar, and cease to pervert our ways. If you refuse, you will still cease speaking of Christ, because I will sentence you to death and order your head to be removed by the executioner's sword before the sun sets, and I will eradicate from Rome those that have followed your babblings.

"But, unlike my stepfather Claudius Caesar, I won't just force Jews and followers of Christ from Rome, I will make an example of these seditionists with like crosses on which your Christ died. Trouble is stirring up against Roman rule again in Judea and I believe you Jews and followers of Christ are the ones that set Rome ablaze according to the teaching of Peter, imprisoned with you, as reported to me, that God will destroy this world with fire. Moreover, I have seen a copy of your seditious dispatch to your followers in Thessalonica in the province of Macedonia, saying your Christ will return in flaming fire to take vengeance on those that don't know your God, and who don't obey your message concerning Christ. You are condemned by your own words seeking to overthrow me, Nero Caesar, and the Empire of the People and Senate of Rome."

Paul answered, "Caesar, I am not careful to answer you even at the cost of my life. I give witness here that Jesus Christ is Lord of all and is over all. To Him every knee will bow and every tongue confess that He is Lord."

Peter's Upside Down Crucifixion

Upon that profession, Nero ordered Paul removed from his sight to be executed outside the city walls and then summoned Peter from the Mamertine Prison to hear his sentence. After a similarly swift hearing before Nero, Peter too was sentenced to death. Nero thought, Rome had put to death the one called Christ and now, with the executions of the most noted messengers of the Christ, an end would be put to what he saw as trouble in the world.

Peter was marched to Nero's private racing circuit near a necropolis. Mark followed at a distance. There in the center of the circuit was a huge obelisk commissioned by the Egyptian Pharaoh Rameses II, whom Moses defeated with the miracles of God. It had been brought from Egypt by Augustus Caesar and dedicated to the sun god, whom Nero tried to emulate. Not feeling worthy to be crucified in the same manner as was the Lord Jesus, Peter requested that he be crucified upside down. There, painfully nailed to a cross, Peter looked at the world he now viewed upside down. He also saw his protégé Mark grieving and perched on a tomb in the necropolis nearby. He prayed that God would preserve Mark and use Mark and others of his generation and generations to come to carry their crosses and continue to turn the world upside down with the message that Jesus is the Christ, the Son of the Living God, come to earth as a man, born of a virgin by the Holy Spirit, proved His ministry by word and miraculous deeds, willingly died a perfect sacrifice for the sins of the world, rose from the dead as the scriptures foretold, ascended back into heaven after appearing to His followers, and is the savior of all who receive Him by faith and openly confess Him.

A Marker on the Ground in Vatican City Located on the left side of Saint Peter's Basilica, Indicating the Original Location of the Obelisk where Peter was Executed in Nero's Racing Circuit and likely the last thing Peter saw as he was Crucified Upside Down.

The Obelisk of Rameses II in Saint Peter's Square, Vatican City.

Paul Finishes His Course, But the Struggle Against Darkness Continues
As Paul was marched from the Mamertine Prison beyond the walls of
Rome, Timothy, Luke, and Onesiphorus followed at some distance as
they journeyed along the Appian Way. As Paul was led and his three
co-workers in the gospel followed, other believers, weeping, joined them
following behind, until Paul was made to kneel in the road and bend his
neck to receive the blow from the executioner's sword.

Although shaken by witnessing the execution of his spiritual father, Timothy recalled Paul's words to him in his final letter to him. He determined to meet with Mark to safely depart Rome and be good soldiers in proclaiming the message of the gospel and building up the churches as God continued the work, through them and others, turning the world upside down by preaching the gospel of Jesus Christ. In so doing, they would fearlessly continue the work of defeating the powers of darkness, upsetting the current order, and establishing the new order of the Kingdom of God and of His Christ from Jerusalem to the uttermost parts of the earth.

ABOUT THE AUTHOR

Louis McCall was born in Chicago, Illinois, and attended Northwestern University, where he received a PhD in political science. Later, he also attended the National War College of the National Defense University. Louis was an Assistant Professor at the Ohio State University in the Department of Political Science prior to a thirty-six-year career in the U.S. Department of State, first as a Foreign Service officer and then as a foreign affairs Civil Service employee where he served as Consul General in Florence, Italy, Chargé d'Affaires in Brunei, U.S. Representative to the Republic of San Marino, and Assistant Inspector General. He lived in or worked in, at least temporarily, more than sixty countries on six continents.

Whether in academia or as a diplomat, Louis found opportunities to live his faith, including part-time ministry of the good news in word and in song, including co-laboring with missionaries, national church leaders, and the underground church. When ministering early in his diplomatic career from the pulpit of a great church in Calcutta, India, Louis said to those in attendance that he had determined not to be ashamed of the gospel of Christ. That has been a commitment he has endeavored to keep over the years. In his final two years at the Department of State, he organized and led the National Day of Prayer observances in the Department.

Now, in his new career as an author, he has the pleasure of greater freedom in sharing what God has placed in his heart. Louis is active simultaneously in two churches in Washington, D.C. One is a multi-site non-denominational church, and the other a Catholic church where he is a regular cantor, though not a Catholic himself.

He has managed this with the blessing and full knowledge of pastors and priests. This has been an outgrowth of his early association with a mixed protestant-Catholic charismatic house-based worship group, his association with the late Saint Mother Teresa of Calcutta, his charismatic Catholic wife, Lenora, and guest ministry in churches and bible schools of various denominations while living in or working in other countries.

Louis is the author of *According to Your Word Lord, I Pray*; *The Epic of God*; and *He Chose the Glory*.

I truly hope you enjoyed this book. It was written for you. Please recommend it to others. I also welcome your feedback. It would really encourage me to hear from you. You can follow me on my website and on social media using the links below.

Website: http://www.louismccallinternational.com
Address: Louis McCall International, PO Box 60211, Washington, DC 20039
Twitter: @DrLouisMcCall
Facebook: www.facebook.com/louismccallinternational